Praise for the Destination: Desire series

"I loved this amazing, emotional love story... A tear or two became commonplace during some intense scenes. In Ms. Jordan's talented hands, the characters evolved naturally and realistically, flaws and all." *-Harlequin Junkie Reviews*

"5 stars. My favorite in the series so far. I just loved the back story of this couple and it's just a different twist on a romance. Loved it!" *-Kristi Simonsen*

"This is an well written story, where you get invested in the characters and root for them to have their HEA...I cannot wait to see what comes next in this series. 5 stars" *-Gigi Staub*

"This was a fabulous story with great characters... one of the best I've read this year. I LOVED this." *-Jennifer McKenzie*

MAYBE
THIS TIME

DESTINATION: DESIRE
BOOK 3

C. JORDAN

CJ BOOKS

contents

Dedication

For Kristi Simonsen, Patsy Hughes, and KittyKelly, because these ladies are awesome and were willing to beta read this book (and the prequel) at lightning speeds.

For the real couple that inspired Valentina and Giovanni, who shall remain nameless to protect *my* innocence. They're every bit as funny, passionate and outrageous in real life as they are in my story. Wishing them both *la dolce vita*.

For the Professor Moriarty, because he's got a solid sense of humor and a sarcastic streak a mile wide. A little bit of him goes into all my heroes.

For the Mad Madam M, because no one does best friend with quite the same flare she does. A little bit of her goes into all my BFF characters.

For Grams, because I miss you every damn day. If you've got phones up there in heaven, give me a call and we'll catch up, okay?

CHaPTer one

Half Moon Bay, California

"So, are you going to change your last name back to Hudson?" Ben asked.

Karen froze at the question from her younger brother. A group of her closest friends and their siblings had come over to her new apartment to help her move in and unpack. They all knew why the move was happening, but only Ben had the temerity to ask about her imploding marriage. Even her friend Anne, who was usually as in-your-face as a person could get, had had the graciousness not to probe that wound too deeply. And if Anne was being circumspect, you knew it was bad.

"Jesus, Ben, really?" Nora—one of Anne's three quirky younger sisters—punched him in the shoulder.

"What?" His brows snapped together, and he rubbed his arm. "It's an honest question. It's not like I didn't ask her how she was doing and everything."

She rolled her eyes. "Still, that's really what you want to ask immediately after your sister"—her voice dropped to a whisper loud enough to be heard two counties over—"files for divorce? You're so sensitive."

"You're so sensitive," he fired back. "No wonder you're a psych major. You have to feel your feelings about every damn thing."

She flushed scarlet and jammed her hands down on her hips. "I switched my major to nursing, jackass."

Ben already had his mouth open to retort, so Karen figured it was time to wade into the fray. Those two had been at loggerheads since junior high, and it showed no sign of stopping even though they were both in their mid-twenties. "Okay, guys. Knock it off or I'm giving you a time out and making you stand with your noses in separate corners."

Anne snickered from where she knelt on the living room floor amidst a sea of half-empty boxes. Their other best friends, Meg and Julie, ducked their heads in from the bedroom.

Julie said, "I'm so glad I'm an only child."

Meg elbowed her in the ribs. "Uh...where do you want us to stick the sweaters and winter clothes?"

Not to be denied his parting shot, Ben turned back to Nora. "Besides, what was I supposed to do? Talk about the weather?"

Sighing, Nora shook her head as if his stupidity saddened her. "Sure, that would have worked better. But maybe tell her that her hair looks awesome instead of reminding her about...stuff."

Stuff being the breakup, the divorce, the end of life as Karen had known it for the last eight years. Stuff being where she went from being Mrs. Tate Patton to Ms. Karen Hudson again. Nope, she absolutely did not want to talk about that. So she fluffed the textured layers of her recently shortened crop. Her once mid-back-length blonde hair now ended just below her chin, and instead of straightening it to perfection as she'd been doing for years, the mussed style took advantage of her natural wave. Maybe the hair reflected the new Karen, because she was tired of pretending to be perfect—that her life was perfect, that cool, calm perfection was even something she wanted. A little muss was just fine with her.

"It really does look nice, sis. Totally different." He winked. "I'm guessing that's what you wanted."

"Yep." To prevent further outbursts between Nora and her brother, she gave him a smile. "Why don't you go down to the moving truck and see if Finn and Lukas need a hand with the heavy lifting? Leave the unpacking to us."

Finn and Lukas were Meg's and Julie's boyfriends, both of whom had been roped into helping and hadn't complained once about the unpaid labor. It made this day both easier and harder that everyone was being so nice and tiptoeing around Karen's feelings. She was just happy her parents were out of town on an extended vacation—them being here adding their quiet sympathy and support to everyone else's would have made it that much worse.

"I'm happy to assist in the estrogen-free zone." Ben was out the door in seconds, though he cast a baleful glance back at Nora before he disappeared.

Nora snorted. "Estrogen-free zone, my ass. No wonder he doesn't have a girlfriend. He's probably still a virgin because he can't be *nice* long enough to get laid."

"Whoa!" Karen slapped her hands over her ears. "I do not want to speculate about my brother's sex life."

"Or lack thereof," added Anne. She gave her sister a pointed look. "Now who's being insensitive?"

"Heh. Me." Nora's grin was abashed. "Sorry, Karen."

Karen was thankfully spared further discussion when Anne's other sisters, Hazel and Camille, tromped in with Chinese food for lunch.

Not that things were likely to settle down upon their arrival. The sisters together in the same room was often like fire, gasoline, and a dry forest just waiting to explode into flames. Anne played referee with that trio so often she could go pro.

"Put the bags on the table, girls." Karen cleared a spot wide enough for the multitude of white cartons. "And go call the guys."

Her brother would have to come back to the estrogen minefield, but he'd need to brave it if he wanted to get fed.

Meg fetched paper plates and Anne rooted around in the boxes until she came up with a set of mismatched silverware. It wasn't the sleek, expensive set Karen and Tate had gotten as a wedding present, but Karen was just as happy not to have the reminder of all her dreams turning to dust.

She tried to paste on a smile for everyone, but it got harder as the day progressed. All her belongings were unpacked and put away. Her new life was in order. She even had a job lined up as director of the Half Moon Bay Public Library. A step up from assistant director at the main library in Palo Alto. She started in two weeks. Everything was going smoothly, so she shouldn't have any complaints.

But how could she feel happy about the dissolution of the life she'd wanted so badly? She'd had something so amazing and wonderful in her grasp, but it had soured and she'd had to let it go or turn sour herself. That didn't mean she was happier for the loss.

If only Tate had—

No, she wasn't letting that awful merry-go-round spin in her head again. They'd been in sync when they'd married, but had grown apart, had wanted different things. She'd wanted a family and had let him put it off until he finished law school, until he'd established his career, until he'd made partner, but eventually she'd realized that he just didn't want what she wanted, no matter what he might claim. He wanted to be married to his job, and she couldn't compete with his corporate mistress. So, she'd gotten out before she went from anger to hate. She didn't want to hate anyone, but she needed to be loved and wanted and fulfilled and Tate didn't have the time to give her that.

Maybe someday she'd find a man on the same wavelength she was, but she didn't have to wait around for him to start a family. She was thirty-three, and while that wasn't old, her chances of conceiving would begin to drop after thirty-five. Only two years away. If she waited and then couldn't have children, she'd regret it forever. Yes, she'd always imagined having Tate's children, but that wasn't going to happen and she had to move on. No more sitting around hoping her life would turn out the way she wanted. Time to make it happen. So, she had an appointment next month with a sperm bank. It had taken a lot of courage to make that appointment, another break from the life she thought she'd have. Her friends had already volunteered to go with her and help figure out which sperm donor to pick.

She really did have awesome friends.

After dinner, she sent the younger siblings back to their respective college campuses. Finn had gone off to return the rental truck and Lukas had followed in his car to bring the other man back. Which left Karen alone with her best friends.

Anne angled a glance at her. "Want us to do a sleepover for this first night?" ·

"We're totally willing," Julie quickly added. She pointed to Meg. "We already cleared it with the guys. Say the word, and Lukas will just drop Finn off at home instead of bringing him here."

Karen arched her eyebrows. "You don't have clothes with you."

"That wouldn't stop us." Meg shrugged, enough empathy in her gaze to make Karen's throat clog.

Moisture burned the backs of her eyes, and she had to blink fast to keep the tears from falling. No more crying. She'd done enough of that since she'd told her husband it was over. Sucking in a deep breath, she shook her head. "No, I think I need to rip the Band-Aid off and just do it."

It had been a decade since she'd slept alone in a house, except the handful of times Tate or she had gone out of town for work. She needed to get this over with, start to make this her routine. And it wasn't as if she'd be alone forever. If she were lucky, by this time next year, she'd have her hands full with a baby. Hard to feel alone when your roommate doesn't let you sleep through the night.

Julie shrugged. "I had a feeling you'd say that."

"Okay, but we're only a few minutes away if you need us for anything," Meg said.

"Seriously, Karen," Anne insisted. "Anything. A cup of sugar, company...borrowing from my extensive porn collection."

A round of groans spilled from the group.

"I'm just kidding! How would I have hidden a collection like that from the girls? They got into everything growing up." Anne ruffled a hand over her short red hair. "Besides, remember I live with the drama mama. You think I want her coming along to knock while I have that stuff playing?" She shuddered. "No thank you."

"She has a point." Karen had camped out on Anne's couch for the first few weeks after the breakup, and she had gained a new appreciation for her friend's restraint in not killing her mother all these years. Karen was usually pretty even-tempered, but the drama llama mama could drive anyone to homicide.

Julie's nose wrinkled. "I don't even want to think about anyone but Lukas walking in on my lady time. I'm just saying. Gross."

"Finn likes watching my lady time." Meg flashed a wicked grin, even as a blush rushed up her cheeks.

A very juvenile round of hooting erupted from everyone, and Karen wanted to hug them. She wouldn't have gotten through this without them, certainly not without having a major mental breakdown. They made her laugh when all she'd wanted to do was cry. They'd helped her keep perspective.

"I love you guys." She looped her arms around Julie's and Anne's waists. Meg crowded in for a tangled group embrace. They held tight for a long time, and the support felt so good—a bulwark of strength she could always depend on, that would see her through everything. Even divorce. "You guys really are the best, you know that, right?"

"'Course we know," Anne said gruffly, then ruined the tough act by giving a little sniffle. She pulled back and scrubbed a hand over her eyes.

Meg and Julie looked a bit teary too.

"Love you too." Meg went to grab a tissue. "We don't say it that often, but still. It's good to have you, even when you're being nosy and bossy."

"We're only nosy 'cause we care." Julie gave a lopsided grin, her eyes welling. "And I wouldn't have survived losing my Auntie Eloise without you girls. Thanks."

"Okay, let's pull it together or we'll scare the guys when they come back." Karen took a tissue Meg proffered and dabbed at her eyes. She pulled in a breath. "Let's meet for breakfast at the Moonside Café. I'll be okay on my own tonight."

"If you change your mind, the sleepover offer stands for tomorrow night or the night after." Anne waggled her eyebrows. "The porn offer already expired though."

"I think I'll survive the disappointment." Karen patted the redhead's shoulder.

A knock sounded on the door, then Finn poked his head in. His gaze lit on Meg and a smile spread across his lips. "Ready to go, honey?"

"Yeah."

He glanced at Julie. "Lukas couldn't find a parking space, so he's stuck in a red zone. He's waiting for you...if you're not having a girls' night." His eyebrows rose as he turned to Karen.

"Nope, they're all yours." Karen gave a magnanimous wave. "Thanks for all your help today."

He shrugged easily. "Any time. Happy to lend a hand."

An hour after they'd gone, Karen was still wandering around her apartment listlessly. She'd straightened pillows that didn't need it, checked cupboards that were neat and organized. Loneliness swamped her, which was ridiculous because if she were still living in their very expensive house in Palo Alto, Tate wouldn't even have been home from his law firm yet. His father would have insisted they stay longer, and Tate would have thrown himself into whatever case they were working on, and it would have been midnight before he crawled into bed beside his wife. She'd be lonely if she were there too. In the end, she thought that might have been what had done her in. Being in a marriage by yourself was a kind of hellish helplessness she wouldn't wish on her worst enemy.

Even this apartment's echoing aloneness was better. A sad, but true statement on her life.

For a moment, she considered calling Anne and asking her to come over. Unlike their other two friends, Anne was single and wouldn't have scheduled a date for tonight. Karen picked up her cell phone, her finger hovering over the speed dial that would connect her to the other woman.

No.

She stiffened her spine. This was the path she'd chosen and she needed to live with it. Alone. If that meant she'd spend the next two weeks crawling the walls between now and the start of her new job, then so be it. The antsy restlessness was annoying, but it would get better. It had to. Gritting her teeth, she moved to set the phone down when it blared out a ring.

Her heart leapt and her fingers clenched on the plastic so hard it squeaked. She pressed a hand to her chest and checked the screen to see who was calling. Brows arching in surprise, she smiled and accepted the call. "Valentina De Rossi, as I live and breathe."

"Karen, darling!" The other woman's musical Italian accent made Karen's name sound more exotic than it was. "I have the most wonderful news."

"Oh? Tell me." Karen smiled at Valentina's effusion. They'd met during Karen's junior year of college when she'd studied abroad in Rome, and had managed to become friends despite their wildly disparate personalities. Her smile faded. Unfortunately, that was also the year she'd met Tate, who'd been in Italy on foreign exchange too. Those lovely Roman memories she'd cherished had suddenly become a bit tarnished.

"Welllll," Valentina said, drawing the word out. "You know I've kept my Giovanni in suspense for quite some time."

"Only over a decade, but who's counting?"

In fact, Tate and Karen had been the ones to introduce Valentina to Giovanni. Another reminder she didn't want, but she shoved that away. It wasn't Gio or Valentina's fault that Karen was getting a divorce.

A tinkling laugh came through the phone. "I finally said yes! We're getting married next week."

"Next week?" Karen echoed.

"I know, it is rash and unplanned and exciting. Just as I like things.

I was always so petrified of the huge wedding and all the planning and details that must be just so. And my mother and aunts and cousins...darling, you know how passionate the Italians are." She sighed dramatically. "There would be fighting. I didn't want the headache. But, my Gio, he knows me. He said I wouldn't be happy eloping because my family wouldn't be there, even though they drive me crazy. So he said our engagement will be very short—not enough time for huge planning or fighting. Just throw the kind of party I love with an even more beautiful and expensive dress."

Curling into the recliner in her living room, Karen grinned. "It was him offering you carte blanche on the expensive dress that convinced you, wasn't it?"

Valentina laughed. "It's entirely possible."

"He knows you so well," Karen murmured. She'd always liked Gio. He was every bit as passionate as Valentina, though with slightly less drama. Valentina was two handfuls, but he was stubborn enough to have hung on. Once he'd decided she was the one he wanted, that was the end of the discussion.

Karen hated to make comparisons between Gio and Tate on that score, but it was hard. Especially when she listened to her friend gush while she was sitting alone in an apartment because Tate had wanted everything else more than he'd wanted to keep her. For Gio, Valentina had always been the priority.

Karen shoved away the petty jealousy that wanted to consume her. No. What kind of friend would she be if she couldn't get past her own issues to be thrilled for two people who had always been genuinely kind to her? Gio and Valentina had come to visit several times over the years. Gio's investment firm had a branch in San Francisco, and he'd been sent on business trips which the couple had turned into vacations.

Valentina hesitated. "I know...things haven't been going so well for you lately." A graceful sidestep from mentioning the divorce. "But I had to share my happiness with someone who was there at the very beginning."

"I am happy for you. Both of you." And she was. Her own situation had nothing to do with theirs. "This is such good news."

Another small pause, and then Valentina's normal exuberance burst out. "Can you come? You must come. Please say you'll come."

Karen looked around her apartment, imagining how two weeks of sitting here by herself would feel. Like the walls were closing in on her. It wasn't as if she couldn't afford the trip. She hadn't spent a dime of her librarian salary in eight years, and even modest earnings added up after that much time. They'd lived off of Tate's income except the chunk of his trust fund they'd used to buy their house.

Besides, when was the last time she'd gone anywhere? Tate had always been too busy to go on vacation and she hadn't felt like going without him. So, she had two weeks off and a very good reason to get out of town. She took a breath. "I'll come."

"Really?" The delight and disbelief that came through the line made Karen grin. She heard Valentina clap her hands. "*Magnifico!* Let me know when you'll arrive and I'll have Giovanni pick you up from the airport."

"I will. Thanks for thinking of me, Valentina."

"Of course, of course!"

Once they were off the phone, Karen punched the speed dial to connect to Anne.

She picked up on the first ring. "Need me to come over?"

"No, and I don't want your porn collection either." Karen propped her feet on the ottoman in front of her chair. "What I need is a ride to SFO."

G od, he was exhausted. Tate couldn't remember ever being so bone-tired in his entire life. His eyes were gritty and burned as he pulled into the driveway of his house. The windows were dark, a harsh reminder that no one was there waiting for him. Empty. A perfect echo of how he felt. Empty, cold, numb. He sat there and stared for a long time before he shifted the car into park, grabbed his briefcase and got out to walk toward that barren cavern of a house.

It felt like a million-pound iceberg pressed down on his chest. A cold, relentless weight he'd carried since that last horrible fight where Karen had finally walked away.

He swallowed, fetched the mail from the mailbox and forced himself to go inside and turn on the lights. The place was spotless, mostly because he was never there. Even less so now that he had no one to come home to.

Setting his briefcase on the kitchen island, he glanced around. Everywhere he looked reminded him of Karen. The round table she'd tucked under the window, the pale yellow she'd painted the walls, the symphony schedule she'd stuck on the refrigerator. Hell, he didn't remember the last time he'd managed to make it to the symphony.

Which had been her point when she'd left. He couldn't even argue with her—he just didn't know how to fix the situation.

Too late now.

When it came to his work and his marriage, he'd been crushed between the proverbial rock and hard place for years. Something had to give, and there'd been times he thought it might be his sanity. He shoved a hand through his hair and went to grab a beer from the fridge. He hadn't found time to eat dinner, but it was after 9pm and he wasn't hungry anymore.

He popped the bottle's top and took a deep swig. The cold bitter brew washed down his parched throat. Sighing, he tried not to notice the silence in the house. He'd brought this on himself, so he had no right to complain. He clung to the numbness inside, knowing the alternative would be far worse. In this case, he didn't want to feel anything, didn't want to think too hard or examine his life too deeply. Only then might he hold the crippling agony at bay.

Everyone had their coping mechanisms.

The phone in his pocket rang and he pulled it out. The screen read *Giovanni* and the first smile of the day touched Tate's lips. The movement almost felt stiff and awkward, as if he hadn't smiled in a hundred years. "Hello?"

"Tate, *mio amico!*"

The grin grew a little bigger. It had been a while since anyone had been enthused to talk to him. "Hey, Gio. How's it going?"

"*Buono.*" A chuckle came through the phone. "Valentina has finally agreed to be my wife."

"She made you work for it," Tate commented. In his experience, Valentina De Rossi was ten pounds of crazy in a five-pound bag. The fun kind of crazy, but still. She was dizzying in her mood changes and effusive in her charm. Tate had always preferred Karen's more understated appeal. Not that he'd made sure she knew it lately, but that hardly mattered now. She was gone and she wasn't coming back.

Gio made a dismissive sound. "My Valentina, she was worth the wait."

Tate's phone beeped and he held it away from his ear to see it was his father trying to get through to him. He ignored the call. Not that it would stop his dad—he'd just call back. Likely it was something he wanted for the office, some case he wanted to discuss, some issue that had just occurred to him. Tate loved his work, but his father could be on the obsessive side. Dad lived for his work and expected Tate to be the same way. Most of the time, he didn't mind, but today it felt like harassment. It was the third call since his father had left the office at 7:30pm. And it was Saturday.

Tapping the button to ignore the other call, he refocused on Giovanni. "So, when's the big day?"

"One week from today." There was a pause. "Oh, it's Sunday here. Still Saturday there, yes?"

"For a few more hours." Tate scooped up the mail and took it and his beer into his office. One of the few rooms that didn't remind him of his erstwhile wife.

"I want you to come," Gio insisted. "I know it's short notice. I know, you're busy. Always so busy, but it's my wedding! You introduced me to my Valentina. I want you there."

"Well, I—"

But a response really wasn't needed because Gio launched into a one-sided argument about all the reasons Tate needed to come to Italy.

Dropping the pile of mail on his desk, Tate pinned the phone between his shoulder and his ear so he could sort through the stack. Bill, bill, junk mail, junk mail, bill, and then a heavy letter with a law firm he recognized on the return address. He frowned. Why would this be delivered here? Legal mail went to his work. After sliding his finger under the flap, he opened the envelope and pulled out the thick sheaf of papers to read.

Gio kept rambling in his ear about the wedding while Tate slowly sank into his chair, the breath wheezing out of him as if he'd been gut-punched.

Petition for Dissolution of Marriage.

He was a lawyer—he'd seen divorce papers many times in his career.

But this petition had his name on it. His and Karen's. That was something he'd never thought he'd see, never wanted to see.

He needed to read these, sign them and get them back to her lawyer.

The line beeped again, and he didn't even have to look to know it was his father. Wanting something, expecting something. Never slowing down or easing up for a single fucking second of the day. And never satisfied unless Tate was giving a thousand percent of his time and energy.

Suddenly it was all too much. The final straw. Every single thing in his life was more than he could take. It was as if a switch had flipped in his head and all he wanted was out.

Without thinking, he stood, went upstairs to his room and pulled out a suitcase. "You know what, Gio? I wouldn't miss your wedding for anything. I'll be there tomorrow. Let me email you the details once I've booked my ticket."

And so, for at least a little while, he'd avoid having to deal with the reality of his life and his marriage—or rather, his divorce.

CHAPTER TWO

Rome, Italy

She'd forgotten how vibrant the city was, especially the narrow, sloping alleys that made up the *Trastevere rione* where she'd gone to college and where Valentina and Gio still lived. Karen had always loved it here. The rush of cars at a breakneck speed they'd never dare in America, the mass of people from all over the world who'd come to visit, the historic architecture, museums, and monuments. She dragged in a breath...and the tantalizing aroma of Italian food hit her nose. There was a restaurant on the bottom floor of Gio and Valentina's building. Karen's mouth watered, her stomach growled and she was forcefully reminded that it would be breakfast time if she were in California. A nine-hour time difference could really mess a body up.

Her old friends lived on the top floor, so Karen had stepped outside on the balcony to escape the wedding preparation madness. She was fairly certain every single female relative of Valentina's had managed to cram themselves into the apartment. And they were loud and boisterous and happy. But mostly loud. Propping her elbows on the railing, Karen looked out over the skyline. A thousand different levels of rooflines, a few cathedral *duomos*, and she could just see the Vatican peeking between some of the buildings. So different from what she was used to.

A wave of laughter spilled out of the apartment, and she glanced back with a grin. They were a nice family—one who'd welcomed her for every holiday during the year she'd spent in Rome. Glancing at her watch, she saw it was well past time when she could check into her hotel.

It took her another half an hour to say goodbye to everyone because they all insisted on a hug and a kiss from her, told her how beautiful she was, how much they liked her new hairstyle, insisted she come back and join them for dinner. Finally, Valentina laughed, grabbed Karen's elbow and thrust her out the door or she might never have escaped. She was still grinning when she hit the bottom of the staircase and entered the lobby.

And slammed into someone trying to go up the stairs. She stumbled back, an apology on her lips, but it never formed as her gaze collided with her soon-to-be-ex-husband's.

"Tate," she said faintly, falling back another step. "Wh-what are you doing here?"

The flash of utter shock on his face told her he'd had no idea they would both be in Rome either. He cleared his throat and shrugged. "The same thing you are, I'd imagine. Attending an old friend's wedding."

There was no way he'd had any more notice on the invitation than she'd had, which meant he'd done something spontaneous for the first time in years. She crossed her arms. "You dropped everything, just like that? You?"

He snorted. "Got one too many calls from Dad the night Gio invited me, so I ran away from home."

The mere glimmer of a smile crossed her lips. "About time."

Shaking his head, he huffed out a laugh. His gaze flitted over her. "You changed your hair."

"Yes." She flicked the tips with her fingers. "A new look to start my new life. I like it."

He winced. She tried not to cringe because, really, she hadn't meant to rub his face in it. It was just the standard response she'd come up with every time someone asked why she'd cut it.

Then there was an awkward moment where she had no idea what to say. She hadn't expected to see him, didn't have a list of banal conversational topics ready to save her from uncomfortable silences. "Uh...okay." She glanced aside. "I need to go check in to my hotel. I, um, guess I'll see you at dinner tonight."

"Yes." He let her get halfway across the lobby before he called out. "Out of curiosity, which hotel are you staying at?"

"The Gianicolo."

"Me too." An ironic smile tilted up one corner of his mouth. "Giovanni recommended it to you too, huh?"

She pressed the tips of her fingers against her temple and rubbed at the building pain. "I may have to murder him."

"Not if I beat you to it." A muscle ticked in his jaw, and he waved her off. "See you at dinner."

"Bye."

Then they went their separate ways. As usual.

S he looked so damn beautiful, she took his breath away. Tate stood there and watched Karen exit the lobby, his gaze moving over every familiar curve of her figure. A searing, awful sensation opened in the pit of his stomach and he wanted to bend over and howl at the pain that shredded his insides. There went the ice that had encased his heart, shattered, until nothing but the agony remained. It rushed up to consume him.

His marriage was over. Because he'd turned into his father. Something he'd always promised himself he'd never do. He'd managed to lie to himself, to cling to some sense of denial until right this very second.

But like his father, he'd become a man so obsessed with his career that he never noticed—or maybe never cared—that his marriage had crumbled. Only his mother hadn't left. No, she spent her afternoons with whatever tennis instructor or masseuse or pool boy had caught her eye. Why not enjoy herself when her husband so clearly didn't want her for anything other than the occasional soiree to wine and dine clients? And Tate was absolutely certain his father was banging one of their first-year law associates. Just like he'd taken his pick of the litter last year and the year before.

Grasping the handrail on the stairs for balance, Tate sat down heavily on the third step. He swallowed hard. He'd told himself when he joined the family law firm—a firm started by his great-grandfather—that Karen and he wouldn't end up like his parents. He'd never once considered touching another woman in all the years they were married, and Karen knew it. And he knew she wouldn't stray either. But fidelity wasn't enough, was it? He'd never heard his parents fight the way he had with Karen. Maybe because his mother didn't fight to save her marriage the way Karen had.

He winced at the thought, but it was the painful truth.

Maybe his parents had started out faithful and loving, though he had difficulty picturing it. They'd been distant strangers living in the same house for as far back as his memory would stretch. All he'd known was that he didn't want that.

But he'd come so damn close to turning his marriage into that, hadn't he? If Karen hadn't walked away, if she'd stayed another five or ten years, would they have turned into indifferent acquaintances who happened to be married?

Probably.

"Tate." Giovanni's voice pulled him back to the present. "What are you doing sitting here? Are you all right?"

The other man crouched before Tate, a concerned expression on his face. Tate's jaw worked, his hands balling into fists on his thighs. When he spoke, his tone was low and controlled. "I could kill you."

Gio leaned back a little. "Ah. So you've seen Karen."

"Ran into her. Literally."

"And it knocked you on your ass?" A knowing smirk curled his lips.

"You know we're divorcing. You had no right to do this to her. Or me." Tate could feel a muscle twitch in his cheek. "We deserved the courtesy of a warning so we could decide if we didn't want to come if our ex-spouse was here."

"Not ex yet." Gio pushed to his feet and crossed his arms over his chest. "You are still married."

"A technicality. She left me. And she was right to do it." Tate swallowed hard, looked his friend in the eye and admitted what he'd refused to ever acknowledge during all the arguments with Karen. "I screwed up our marriage. I made everything except her a priority because I assumed she'd always be there when I needed her. But I wasn't there when she needed me. I took her for granted and so I lost her. It's my fault. It's all my fault."

The Italian shrugged. "So fix it."

A laugh strangled out of Tate, and he felt the humiliating burn of moisture at the back of his eyes. "You can't undo eight years of stupidity and neglect overnight, Gio. And if she has any sense of self-preservation at all—which she does, trust me—she wouldn't even consider giving me a second chance."

"Have you asked her?" Gio's brow rose, daring Tate to give him an answer.

"I don't deserve it," he replied quietly. "And you shouldn't have arranged for this meeting without consulting us." He blew out a breath. "I probably shouldn't stay."

An utterly offended expression crossed his friend's face. "You cannot leave now. You'd break Valentina's heart. You'd make Karen have to answer questions from the whole family. And Italian women, they don't let things go. Karen will have to spend the next week—no, ten days—talking about you. If you stay, she can ignore you or not as she chooses."

"Yes, and there won't be any questions then, I'm sure." Tate arched an eyebrow. "That's some backwards logic and you know it."

"I want you here, my friend. Valentina wants Karen here. It is important to both of us that the people who brought us together celebrate our marriage." Gio's hands lifted and dropped. "Don't leave."

Tate rubbed his forehead. He shouldn't stay. He wanted to. Damn, but he wanted to be anywhere Karen was. A sentiment that was far too little and far too late. He should leave her alone. She wouldn't want to spend ten whole days with him around. And there was a certain irony in them both deciding to stay a few days past the wedding. They might even be on the same flight home. He sighed. "I'll stay for the wedding, but no matchmaker stuff. No purposefully throwing us together."

"The wedding preparations might—"

"You know what I mean, Gio. Promise me."

Gio glanced away. "Don't blame Valentina for this. She told me it was foolish to invite you after she'd invited Karen, but..." He clapped a hand over his chest. "I'm a romantic at heart, my friend. I couldn't resist."

"That wasn't a promise."

He gave him a look that was sly and guilty at the same time. "I promise. Nothing deliberate." Gio leaned forward conspiratorially. "But if you'll take some advice, you should use this opportunity to get down on your knees and beg Karen for another chance. You've always looked at her like I look at Valentina. That kind of love, it doesn't die. Not ever."

Tate had the unsettling feeling that his friend was right. No matter how messed up his priorities had been or how often they'd quarreled, he'd never stopped loving her.

Something in his expression must have given him away, because Gio's lips quirked in a smug grin. "You can't deny that you're just a little bit thrilled to see her, can you?"

No, he couldn't deny it, but he wasn't going to admit that to a cocky Italian. There was as much pain as pleasure in seeing her. It was like a knife to the heart to run into her so unexpectedly, and here in Rome where it had all started. Memories had assaulted him from the moment he'd stepped off the plane. He remembered walking these streets with her while they held hands, sitting in a café sipping espresso and talking for hours. The excitement and thrill of new love and passion. It had all seemed so bright then, like nothing could ever break the bond they'd forged here.

A little over a decade later and he was up to his eyeballs in regret.

He'd been so sure that he could have it all. A place in his family's firm, the perfect career, the perfect wife, the perfect life. How arrogant he'd been. How stupid he felt now. Little by little, he'd turned into his father's image. So buried in work there was nothing else in his world, nothing of any real significance. He'd let the most important thing slip through his fingers, the one true thing that had made it worth getting up in the morning.

He was the biggest fool who'd ever lived.

Gio thrust out a hand to help him stand. "Don't give up hope so easily, Tate. Valentina and I have had our share of fights, and we've almost called it quits a couple of times, but we love each other and we've worked it out. If you love a woman, you do what you must to keep her." He waved a hand in Tate's face. "You make it complicated in your head and tell yourself that it's too late, it's hopeless. But it's very simple. A woman like Karen is worth holding on to, worth fighting for. So fight for her."

Fight for her. He snorted. There was something he'd never done. Fight with her? Yes. Fight for her? No. He'd let her walk away without a word of protest, unable to believe she really meant it. Denial again. The reality was, he'd pushed her away. Maybe not on purpose, but hindsight being what it was, he could see how every choice he'd made in the last decade had led him to where he was now.

Alone.

CHAPTER THREE

D inner was a lesson in torment. Valentina's grandmother had pushed Karen into the chair next to Tate...and no one in their right mind argued with that woman. Not to mention, Karen had had no desire to bring more attention to the fact that Tate and she were the antithesis of the happy couple Gio and Valentina presented. Tate cast the occasional glance in Karen's direction, but said little, which should have been comforting, but instead just felt weird. The longer she had to sit next to him, the more surreal the situation became, and the more wine she drank. Not the most mature way to handle things, but she was at a party in Italy. The *vino* flowed freely.

It was well after midnight by the time Gio poured her into a taxi. He all but shoved Tate in after her, who looked none too sober himself. They tumbled out in front of their hotel, and the world tilted oddly in front of her eyes. She blinked hard, trying to focus enough to get in the door.

"Oooooops," Tate said, catching her arm when she staggered. A sweet tingle went down her skin. She frowned. There was a reason that should be a bad thing, but she wasn't really certain what it was. Oh, yes. The divorce.

They bumped into each other a few times on their way to the elevator, and on the fourth bump, she burst into laughter. It echoed in the lobby and she clamped a hand over her mouth, eyes wide. Tate seemed to think that was hilarious because then he laughed too.

"We're loud," she whispered, tilting toward him, then back.

He nodded and pushed the button to call the elevator. They collided when they both tried to enter the car at the same time, which made them chortle.

"Whoops. Manners." Tate waved her in first, then covered his mouth to smother a drunken hiccup. "Ladies first."

"Thanks."

Inside, he stared at the buttons with ferocious concentration. "What floor are you on?"

"The third, but they number things weirdly here," she said knowledgably, proud that she remembered. Right now, she was a bit vague on her own name. "The ground floor is zero."

"Okay. Good." His finger circled the buttons a few times before he managed to hit the right one. "I'm on the third floor too."

"That's nice." She hummed a little song as they began to slide upward. Very slowly. She'd never been in an elevator so slow. The only way she knew they were moving was the dial that pinged over to the next floor.

"I wanted to say...you look really pretty tonight. I like your new hair." He squinted. "Don't know if I told you that before, but I really, really like it. You're beautiful, Karen."

"Thank you. That's so sweet." A silly grin spread on her face, and warmth bloomed inside her.

"I have some prosecco in my room. Got it when I was buying a bottle of wine to bring to dinner." He swayed as the elevator lurched to a stop on their floor. "Want to share a glass with me?"

"Oooh, prosecco." That stuff was like Italian champagne with all kinds of fizzy bubbly goodness. She'd always loved it. "Okay."

A tiny warning bell went off in the back of her head, but she wanted to feel fizzy and bubbly inside, so she ignored it and followed Tate into his room. They bumped into each other again as he tried to turn and shut the door and they both burst into guffaws.

"Shh," he said, the sound slurring. "We don't want to be too loud and get in trouble."

She nodded sagely. "Then we wouldn't get to have prosecco."

A snigger of laughter came from his nose as he reached around her to lock the door. She ended up pressed against the wood, which was good because her balance wasn't too great. Tate's chest slid over hers and that old spark of chemistry that had never really extinguished made her nipples tighten and a rush of heated warmth sluiced down her body. *Mmm,* and didn't that feel nice? She closed her eyes to savor the sensation, a grin tipping up her lips.

"I would *loooove* to know what you're thinking right now." Tate's breath brushed over her neck as he spoke, and it made goose bumps shiver down her skin. That felt nice too. His nose nuzzled into the sensitive spot just below her ear. "You smell so good, Karen."

Her hands rose to press against his shoulders. She should push him away, but she was so tingly it was hard to make herself stop. Her muscles felt like putty, so loose and languid, she let her head fall back against the door. He braced his forearm over her head, leaned into her and their bodies met from knee to chest. The angles of him fit snugly with her curves, and the warmth within her scorched into pure fire. He slid his tongue up her throat and captured her earlobe, dragging a low moan out of her. Her nipples thrust against the lace of her bra, her sex clenching on emptiness. Her legs went weak and, if it weren't for him plastered against her, she'd have slid to the floor.

His fingers skimmed up her sides, leaving ripples of wicked longing in their wake. The hard ridge of his erection nestled into the crux of her thighs, and it was all she could do not to rub against him. He rocked into her, the movement subtle, but enough to stimulate every nerve in her body. Lust swept through her, made it hard to think about anything except what she knew he could do to her.

She licked her lips, tried to summon some self-control. "We're drunk. We shouldn't be doing this."

"Tell me to stop and I will," he whispered. His lips feathered over hers, once, twice, three times. Tempting her, coaxing her to respond. She could be half-dead and she thought she'd respond for this man.

"Um…" She whimpered into his mouth, fighting herself. It was a losing battle. He palmed her breast, and whatever thoughts she had scattered. She wanted, she needed.

"Tell me, Karen," he breathed.

What was she supposed to tell him again? Maybe it was the wine, maybe it was the mindless desire, but everything seemed hazy. When his fingers pinched and rolled her nipple, it felt like a lightning strike of need went from breast to loins. She sucked in a breath, shuddering as she felt her core grow slick. His leg insinuated itself between hers, pulling the skirt of her filmy dress tight, and the hard muscle in his thigh rode against her nub. A sob ripped out of her and she clutched at his shoulders.

Her hips arched of their own volition, seeking that contact. Need throbbed within her, and she could feel herself building toward climax. Oh God. Oh. God. Her nails bit into his arms. "Don't stop."

"I won't." He pulled her forward, stumbling back until he sat on the edge of the mattress. He drew her down so she straddled his lap, her dress bunched up around her thighs. His dark eyes gazed up at her, moving over her face. Threading his fingers through her hair, he offered her a slumberous half-smile that made her burn. "You're so amazingly beautiful."

She felt beautiful when he looked at her like that. "You're not so bad yourself."

"Come here." He tightened his grip on her hair, tugging her downward. His mouth slanted on hers, his tongue thrusting between her lips. One hand slipped around to unzip the back of her dress, and then his fingers were on her skin. She slipped the buttons free on his shirt, wanting to feel him, wanting more.

He peeled her dress down to her waist, and groaned when she unfastened her bra and tossed it aside. His lips closed over one stiff peak, his tongue swirled around her nipple and his teeth grazed the sensitized flesh. She gasped, her back bowing to press herself closer to his talented mouth. "Please."

His fingers trailed up the outside of her thigh, making her shiver. A moan broke from her throat when he slipped his hand between them and rubbed his knuckles over her sex. The thin cotton of her panties was all that kept him from touching her damp folds, and each pass of his hand made desperation scream through her. She was so turned on she was trembling, so frustrated she wanted to cry. He pulled away, and she sobbed.

"I want you naked, sweetheart." He slid his hands under her dress and eased it over her head. "Ah, that's more like it."

She propped her fists on her hips and shook her head slowly. "You must be way more plastered than you think. I am not naked, Tate. I still have my underwear on."

His smile was more than a little tipsy, but he said, "I know how to fix that."

"Oh, yeah?"

He set her on her feet and rose, then toed off his shoes and stripped out of his clothes. She knew she was supposed to get rid of her panties, but instead she watched him undress. God, he was good-looking. Hair and eyes that reminded her of dark chocolate, square jaw, patrician nose and a lower lip that was just a little too full. He was long and lean with the kind of muscle definition that made her want to run her tongue over every ridge and plane.

He sat down to jerk off his socks. "Not sure I can quite manage this standing up."

She kicked aside her heeled sandals, letting her gaze roam over his body. The hard arc of his erection made her insides quiver. He reached out and took her hand, reeling her in. His thumbs hooked over the edge of her panties, tugging them down until they dropped to her ankles.

"Step out of them."

She did as he bid, lifting her feet carefully and holding on to him for balance. If she tilted too far in one direction, she was afraid she'd end up in a heap on the ground. He rested his forehead against the curve of her stomach, the tips of his fingers grazing her inner thighs. She shifted her legs farther apart to give him better access, then clutched at his hair when he stroked over her slick lips. He circled her entrance, then pushed two thick fingers into her sex. She whimpered, rising onto her tiptoes as the sensations grew more intense. Then he moved down to slip his tongue into the thatch of curls between her thighs. The first flick of his tongue over her nub made her jolt, her ankles wobbled, and her legs gave out.

He caught her close, fell back on the bed, and they ended up on their sides facing each other. But desire knifed through her. She needed him. Now. Right now. Slinging her leg over his hip, she pressed as close as possible. The head of his shaft probed at her entrance, and he filled her in one swift plunge.

The exquisite stretch made her choke on a breath. So good. So amazingly good. He palmed her backside, his grip tight as he used the leverage to sink deep. She clung to his shoulder and arched her body, moving with him. Faster and faster, harder and harder. What her body craved was just beyond her grasp, and her muscles burned as she pushed herself to greater speeds. Little gasps spilled from her mouth, sweat slid in rivulets down her flesh.

"Please, please, please." God, she needed surcease.

He reached between them and thumbed her nub in time with their movements. Her sex clenched with every thrust, orgasm rising high and hot within her. When he pinched that tight bundle of nerves, she came in a heated rush, her inner channel milking the length of his shaft. She rode him until she'd wrung every last bit of pleasure out of the experience, her sex pulsing in rhythmic waves that only grew more powerful each time he entered her. It was almost too much, but that was what made it just right. Then she closed her eyes and sighed. Tingles ran over her limbs and euphoria made her grin.

He shifted against her, his erection still a hard presence within her. She lifted her head and frowned at him. "You didn't...?"

"Not yet." He flipped her onto her back, which made her head spin in a dizzying whirl. Wow, she really was drunk. She giggled, then moaned when he surged deeper into her. He cupped his palms over her cheeks, his gaze intent on her face. "This might take a while."

Then he kissed her and started thrusting again. Time seemed to stretch, become elastic, and the world was nothing but sensation. The slide of his hands on her skin, the tactile pleasure of his chest—crisp hair, smooth flesh, taut muscles. The taste of him, spiced with red wine. The scent of Tate and sex and sweat. The creak of the mattress beneath them as they moved, the harsh groans at every touch, the rasp of their breath as they panted for air. The low cries as they crashed into orgasm together.

He reached for her more than once during the night, and her body responded, so high on endorphins she all but purred every time he stroked her skin. She didn't know when they finally passed out, when she slid from post-coital bliss into dreamless slumber. All she knew was that nothing and no one had ever made her feel the way he did. His arm curled around her, he nuzzled his nose in the nape of her neck, and they both sighed as sleep claimed them.

T ate flinched as a piercing shaft of sunlight hit his eyelids.

"Jesus Christ," he muttered and turned his face the other way, trying to blink some of the fog out of his eyes. The inside of his mouth felt like a desert.

An empty bottle of prosecco sat on the bedside table. Hazy memories began to resurface of exactly what had happened here last night. Karen. Him. They'd made love over and over again. He couldn't get enough of her, gorging himself on what he knew he couldn't keep. He recalled pouring the prosecco over her lovely body and sipping the bubbly liquid from her nipples, the valley between her breasts, the hollow of her navel.

The hinges on the bathroom door squeaked and it felt like a nail was shoved into his eardrum. Fuck.

"Fuck." Karen groaned and he watched her stagger into the bedroom.

By pressing the butt of his palm to his forehead, he tried to ease the pounding in his skull. "Good morning."

She squinted. "I think it's afternoon."

Nodding cautiously, he said, "Booze, sex, and jetlag."

A tiny smile wisped across her lips. "All three guaranteed to keep you in bed late."

"Yeah." He sat up slowly, scrubbing a hand through his hair. The blankets were off the bed and the sheets were twisted. "You all right?"

She winced and sighed. "Feeling like an idiot, but fine otherwise."

"Don't," he said softly.

"What?" She glanced around the room, then went to the end of the bed and stepped into her sandals.

"Don't feel like an idiot." Pain shafted into his heart, and it had nothing to do with the hangover. Last night had been amazing. For him, at least.

A snort erupted from her and she tossed a look at him. "Tate, I had a drunken sexfest with a man I'm divorcing. How is that not idiotic?"

He shook his head. "I don't know. I just know I don't regret it. How can you regret the best sex of your life?"

"I think we've done better before." Her lips pursed into a thoughtful moue.

A laugh straggled out of his throat. "I meant sex with you in general was the best I've ever had, not last night specifically."

"Well, I guess one last evening for old time's sake isn't too bad." She sounded like she was trying to reassure herself. Brushing at the wrinkles in her dress, she blew out a breath. "Right?"

"Right. For old time's sake." His lips twisted in a bittersweet smile. "We had a lot of good times in Rome."

"Yeah, we did." Her gaze met his, then shifted away. Some emotion flitted across her face that he couldn't quite read. "Tate...did, um, did we use a condom last night?"

"Not that I recall," he answered cautiously. "I haven't been with anyone else since you left."

Jealousy that he had no right to feel ripped through his insides. Had she slept with other men? She was a single woman now. She could if she wanted to, but the very thought of some other man touching Karen made his head feel as if it might explode.

"Neither have I." She made an impatient gesture. "Condoms are used for more than just disease prevention, Tate."

"You're on the pill." Or, at least, she had been for the eight years of their marriage. Longer, he thought. "Aren't you?"

She shook her head, refusing to meet his gaze. "I...have an appointment next month with a sperm bank, so I went off birth control because, well, I want to get pregnant."

Their last fight had been about that very issue. She had wanted to start a family, he had wanted to wait a bit longer. What he was waiting for, he doubted either of them knew. He'd given her all kinds of excuses, but if he were brutally honest with himself, he'd admit he'd been scared. Scared he'd mess his children up. Scared that he'd be as crappy a parent as his parents had been to his younger sister, Laurel, and him. But Karen could be pregnant with his child right this very moment. His insides squeezed tight. *Yes.* He wanted that. Wanted to see her grow round with his child, wanted to be there for that helpless little human being.

It was an earth-tilting moment. Had he ever really let himself consider if he wanted children, or had he just agreed with Karen that they should have them, and pushed the reality of having them away so he wouldn't have to face his fears? Longing lodged in his chest. For Karen. For the kids they could have together. Could he use this to get her back? He knew the thought was low and totally unworthy of him, but he couldn't stop the way his heart skipped a beat when he thought about it. All he knew was that he wanted back the life he'd thrown away. Wanted a chance to prove to himself—and to Karen—that he could get it right.

Swallowing, he met Karen's gaze. "This...could complicate things."

She cleared her throat. "The timing is wrong for me to get pregnant, but that doesn't mean it's impossible."

"You'll let me know if I got you pregnant." At the very least, it could allow him to drag out their divorce proceedings for a little while, until they knew for sure. Then custody and child support arrangements would need to be made. Of course, he hoped that wouldn't be necessary. Not because he hoped she wasn't pregnant, but because he hoped they'd be reconciled.

"Of course. I'll know one way or the other later this month." She gave the door a vague wave. "I should probably go. I'd rather Valentina and Gio didn't find out about any of this. They'd never let up with the matchmaking if they knew."

Very true, and he didn't want the Italian dynamic duo interfering. He gave Karen as reassuring a look as he could muster. "My lips are sealed."

"Thank you."

"Anything for you."

A spasm of pain crossed her face and the smile she offered him was forced. "Right. Anything for me."

Only he hadn't done anything for her for a long time, had he? He wanted to kick himself for the terrible choice of words.

She turned away and he scrambled to his feet, ignoring the sickening throb in his head. "Karen."

Her hand on the doorknob, she didn't look at him. "Yes?"

Hell, how did he even start this conversation? He was a lawyer. He was supposed to be good at talking people into or out of things. But this was Karen, and she was far more important than any case he'd ever taken to trial. He rubbed sweaty palms down his naked thighs. "If it helps at all, I...have a lot of regrets when it comes to our relationship. I know the divorce is my fault."

He wasn't sure if the sound she made was a laugh or a sob, but it made his heart ache. She glanced over her shoulder at him. "It helps. And it doesn't."

Nodding, he took a step toward her. "I'm sorry."

"Me too." She flipped open the lock on the door. "I have to go now."

"I'll see you later." If he had his way, he'd be seeing her as often as humanly possible in the time they had left in Rome.

She nodded and slipped out.

He wanted to chase her down and beg for a second chance, but knew it would be better to give her some space to think. This morning had been one of stunning clarity for him. All his doubts fell into nothingness. He knew what he wanted for the first time in a very long time. No conflict, no uncertainty. Now he needed to think, to plan. How to get her back, how to make the kind of changes in his life that would make it possible to keep her—and keep her happy. Along with any child they might have together.

His work would always be important to him, but he wanted to live for his family. The work didn't mean a damn thing without the people who mattered. The emptiness that had consumed him since Karen left was proof enough of that. His priorities had been out of whack for a long while, but he had his head on straight now.

Locking the door behind Karen, he headed for the shower. Cleaning up and getting some coffee would go a long way toward making him feel human again. A couple of aspirin would help too. Before he reached the bathroom door, his cell phone blared out. Groaning, he grabbed his head. "Shit."

After swiping the phone off the nightstand, he stabbed the button to accept the call, if only to make it stop ringing. Unfortunately, when he looked at the screen, he cursed again. He pressed the cell to his ear. "Dad."

His father growled, "What the hell are you doing? We're in the middle of an important case."

Tate pinched the bridge of his nose, wishing he'd had a chance to take that aspirin. "We're always in the middle of an important case. You were the lead on this one and you have a small army of lawyers there to help you. You don't need me."

Instead of refuting that, his father shouted, "This is completely irresponsible!"

The sound nearly drove Tate to his knees. His eyeballs felt like they were ready to burst.

"Maybe it is irresponsible." He took a fortifying breath. "But Karen is here, so I'm staying. I have plenty of vacation time saved up. I'm allowed to use it."

"Oh, Jesus," his father groaned. "You never were sensible when it came to her."

Far more sensible than he should have been, which was why he'd lost her in the first place.

"Son, she left you. Don't pant after her like a dog."

He winced at the comparison. "Dad, let me be clear. I'm going to try and get Karen back. When I come home, I'm leaving to start my own firm."

Until he'd said it, he hadn't realized that was what he wanted, but it felt right. If he stayed where he was, it would be far too easy to slide back into old habits. Especially with his father pressuring him to do so.

There was a long pause. "And if you can't get her back? Will you stay with our firm?"

"No. I need to make a break." Tate straightened his shoulders. "As you said, I'm not as sensible as you. I don't want to be married to my work. I want to be married to my wife."

His father blustered, "Your mother and I—"

"Have a pathetic excuse for a relationship." He gave a short laugh. "Don't even go there, Dad."

A harrumph echoed through the phone.

"Goodbye, Dad. I'll see you in a couple of weeks when I clear out my office."

The line clicked as his father hung up on him. It felt like the final break with his old existence. This had been coming for a long time. He just wished he'd figured it out before Karen had given up hope on their relationship. He had no one to blame but himself for that, and now he had to find a way to convince her that he wasn't a hopeless case.

He didn't know how to do that, but he had to try. As Gio had said, Karen was a woman worth fighting for, and that was exactly what Tate intended to do. He'd had her in his arms again last night, and that was where she belonged. He smiled.

Even with the hangover, he hadn't felt this good in months.

CHAPTER FOUR

Karen stumbled down the hotel hallway, wishing for death. Her head was going to implode, throbbing in sickening waves. Oh God. She hadn't drunk that much in a single night...hell, maybe ever. Not even in college. She used one hand to shield her eyes from the glowing wall sconce, fumbling in her purse for her keycard with the other.

After slipping inside her room, she went straight to the shower, washing the scent of sex and Tate off her skin. She deliberately shut her mind down, refusing to think too deeply on what she'd done the night before. As drunk as she'd been, she'd assume her memories would be fuzzy, but there was more than enough clarity to make her want to kick her own ass.

But the irony of possibly getting one-nighter-oopsy pregnant after years of begging Tate to knock her up? Ouch, that burned.

She grabbed a bottle of water, downed a handful of Advil, and carried the hydrating liquid with her to the little desk tucked against the wall. She was going to need a lot of water today. Booting up her laptop meant she could check email and let her friends and family know how she was doing. Of course, she'd have to leave a few pertinent details out.

Suddenly, her computer started chiming loudly, setting off pounding in her temples. She grabbed her forehead and stabbed the button that would accept the Zoom call, but made sure not to activate the video function. Voices only because she was sure she looked like pale death.

"Anne," she groaned.

Her friend bellowed, "Hey, Karen!"

Karen's mouth opened in a silent scream of pain. "Keep your voice to a mere whisper or I will reach through this laptop and rip your vocal cords out."

"Wow, rough night?" Anne murmured. Very, very quietly.

Would the Advil never kick in? Karen massaged her temples. "I spent some quality time with a couple of bottles of red wine. And then a bottle of prosecco."

She could all but see her friend's philosophical shrug. "Well, the post-marital drinking was bound to happen sooner or later."

Ha. As if it were so simple to explain away her boozing. "Giovanni invited Tate too. And Mr. Workaholic Lawyer actually showed up."

"Oh. Damn," Anne breathed. "You're kidding me, right? Tell me that's a bad joke."

"Yep, and the joke is on me," Karen said grimly.

A sound of distress came through the laptop speaker. "Do you want me to—"

"Noooo." She drew the word out. The last thing she wanted was more people involved in this hot Italian mess. "No, I do not want you to do anything other than be your wonderful self, nine time zones away."

"I'm telling Meg and Julie," Anne stated firmly.

Karen rubbed her temples. "I assumed as much."

"How are you doing, honey?" The sympathy in her friend's tone made the feelings she'd been avoiding come bubbling to the surface. The enormity of what she'd done was overwhelming.

Her voice shook a bit. "Promise you'll keep this to yourself?"

"Ah, man." Anne sighed. "You slept with him, huh? Was that before or after the boozefest?"

"During. The wine came first, the prosecco while we were...yeah." Karen bent and pressed her forehead to her knees. She groaned. "Jesus, Anne."

"It's okay, hon. Really. You're hardly the first woman to have a one-nighter with an ex."

"Yeah, if I could just walk away and pretend it didn't happen. Oops, I slipped. But he's still here! We're still here for nine more days."

There was a long pause, and then Anne asked softly, "Is the problem that he's still there or that you still want him?"

A laughed strangled from Karen. "You already know the answer to that one."

"Chemistry can be such a fickle little bitch."

"Yep." She drew in a breath. "There's more."

"Not just Tate? You had a threesome?"

Karen giggled, as Anne had meant her to. But her mirth died a quick death. "No. I—we—there was no condom and I'm not on birth control anymore."

"Cuz you want to get inseminated, right."

Most people would have been shocked speechless, but not Anne. She just took it all in stride. The drama mama had made her immune to everything except a nuclear bomb. Even then, maybe she'd be totally chill about it. Thank God for Anne. That was precisely what Karen needed right now.

"Well, if you get knocked up, you do," Anne said with her usual frankness. "When's your next period supposed to hit?"

"The end of the week. Ish." Karen swallowed, did the same math in her head as she'd done this morning with Tate. It still came out the same. Borderline. "So, it could happen, but I would have been most fertile last week."

"Okay. We'll just have to wait and see. Though I'd lay off the *vino*, just in case. For several reasons."

The risk of harming the maybe-baby and the risk of drunk-jumping Tate again. Awesome. This vacation just got better and better. "Yeah."

"Are you sure you don't want me to tell the other two about this? Let me break it to them so you don't have to? They're gonna wonder what's up if you come home and cancel the sperm bank appointment, but still give birth." Anne drawled, "They know that shit isn't immaculate."

Laughter burst out of Karen. The Advil must have kicked in because it only made her head ache a little. "I love you, Anne. Just so we're clear."

"Totally clear," her friend replied cheerily. "So? Meg and Julie?"

"You can tell them, but they are not to ask about it. At all. Not until I'm ready to talk about it." She hesitated. "Which might be when the maybe-baby is forty."

"Okay, then. Noted. I'll pass that along."

Karen sat back in her chair. "Thanks."

"You sure you don't want me to hop on a plane?" Anne sighed. "You know I'd love an excuse to escape my mom for a while. I can call in sick to work for the first time in my entire career."

"Sorry, sweetie. Tate already took the I-ran-away-from-home slot for this trip."

Karen heard Anne snap her fingers and make a little sound of regret.

"Well, crap. He snaked that right out from under me."

"Any response I have to that is gonna sound wrong and dirty." Karen slid her fingers through her damp hair, loosening the waves. "You should get to bed. It's nighttime there."

"Take care."

"Bye." Tapping a button on her laptop, she closed the connection.

Her stomach gurgled, letting her know it was time for food. By her internal clock, she'd missed a meal or two. Eating something light probably wouldn't be a bad thing—as long as it was bland enough not to upset her stomach. An ironic smile curled her lips. If she was pregnant, bland food was going to be on her menu for several months at least to ward off morning sickness. Well, she might as well get used to it now. If Tate hadn't knocked her up, the sperm bank would.

She dressed and put on the biggest pair of sunglasses she had with her. After grabbing her hat with a wide, floppy brim, she tucked the Advil bottle into her purse and headed out the door. A quick glance told her Tate's door was closed, but he had the tag out saying he wanted his room cleaned, which meant he was probably already gone.

"Whew." She let a breath filter out and took the stairs instead of waiting for the clunky elevator.

The moment she stepped into the lobby, she found Tate speaking to a man in a courier uniform. She pretended not to see them and started to walk past, but Tate's face lit up when he noticed her and her heart did funny things in her chest that made her want to give it a stern talking-to. *Bad heart. Bad.*

"Hey, Ms. Has An English Degree. Can you read this over for typos?" He waved her over and handed her a sheet of paper. She gave it a quick glance, not really interested in being anyone's proofreader today.

Her breath caught when she focused on the words. She slid off her sunglasses and went back to read each sentence carefully. It was a letter of resignation from the Patton law firm. A tangle of emotions gripped her—pain, anger, sadness—and she didn't know which one should win.

Licking her lips, she handed the letter back to him. "It looks fine."

"I should have done this a long time ago." He folded the paper, tucked it into an envelope, and then handed a stack of identical envelopes to the courier. Tate signed a digital pad the other man held out, and that was that. "Done. Those should be delivered to the senior partners of the firm tomorrow. I gave a verbal resignation to my father over the phone earlier, but now it's official."

Since she had no clue what to say about his resignation, she kept her thoughts on his overbearing father to herself. "Robert will be most displeased."

"Dad is displeased no matter what. He's a man who's never satisfied." Tate let out a lungful of air. "You were even concerned about him trying to remake me into his workaholic image when we first got engaged. I had a consuming passion for the law, and he used that to his advantage. And I let him, young idiot that I was. I should never have joined the firm with him in charge."

Karen shrugged. "It was your dream."

That was true. They'd both been determined to have everything they wanted when they first met. They were young, smart, and ambitious. Why shouldn't they be able to have it all? Unfortunately, it just became a tug-o-war between Karen and Robert over Tate's time. Robert had won because Karen had let go. But then, it looked like neither of them had won, had they? Tate had taken himself out of the war. Karen just wished he'd made that decision a year or five ago, but she tucked that pain away. This was the healthiest career choice he'd ever made, so she dug down deep inside and found the strength to be pleased for him, rather than upset for herself.

Tate nodded. "Maybe it was my dream, but not anymore. I'm going to start my own practice."

Wariness slid through her, replacing some of her pleasure. "Competing with your father?"

"Not deliberately." He slipped his hands into the pockets of his khaki shorts, and she realized she was so used to him wearing suits to the office, that this was the most casually dressed she'd seen him in a very long time. He tilted his head. "I don't think I'll stay in Palo Alto, and I'm limiting my client list."

"Where will you go?"

"That remains to be seen." His smile was enigmatic, and his eyes sparkled like he had a secret. "So...how's your head?"

She replaced her sunglasses and set her floppy hat on her head. "I'm trying not to think about it."

"Me too. Have you eaten yet?"

Another little rumble quaked her stomach. "No."

"The concierge recommended a café down the block for good food and very strong espresso." He gestured toward the door. "Want to join me? Caffeine and food will fortify you before you deal with Valentina and the million women in her family."

"She has an impressive number, doesn't she?" Karen stayed where she was for a moment, weighing her options. She was hungry, and he had a nearby place to go. She shouldn't be anywhere near him, but she'd already slept with him, so what would a meal hurt? It wasn't as if she wouldn't be sharing a table with him every time they went to Gio and Valentina's. In the end, practicality and hunger won out.

She gestured for him to lead the way, and other than a tiny glint of triumph in his gaze, he didn't acknowledge any sort of victory in getting her to willingly spend time with him while sober.

He slid on his own sunglasses, walked across the lobby and held the door open for her, then continued their previous conversation. "Valentina has too much of a good thing, I think. I'm suddenly glad it was just Laurel and me growing up and that our parents were only children. No cousins to speak of."

Karen flinched as they hit the bright afternoon sunshine and tugged down her hat brim a bit. "How is your sister?"

"Really good." Affection shone in his voice. "She's got a gallery showing for her paintings at Stanford in a few weeks. I'm sure she invited you."

"She did." She cleared her throat. "I wasn't sure if..."

"Yes, you should go," he said firmly. "Laurel adores you and I know you feel the same. You and I are mature enough to handle being in the same room at the same time. As this week will no doubt prove."

He strode beside her on the sidewalk, and while she was grateful he didn't try to touch her, she could still feel the body heat radiating off him, enveloping her. It reminded her too much of what they'd done together. An unwelcome shiver passed through her. "So...did you kill Gio yet?"

"We had words," he stated dryly. "He was ready to kill me when I threatened to leave."

She made a humming noise. "Yep, you leaving would upset Gio, which would upset Valentina. Upsetting her means those million relatives would hunt you down and finish you off. Sometimes cousins come in handy. I think Italians have a lock on that. Hello, Mafia."

"My sense of self-preservation has spared Giovanni's life. For now."

"They say revenge is a dish best served cold," she agreed.

"While espresso is best served hot." He waved her into a café, and they found a quiet table in a shadowed corner.

Slipping off her sunglasses and hat, she sat back in her seat and looked around. It wasn't a fancy place, but some of the best food she'd tasted in Italy was found in street-side markets and little holes in the wall just like this one. The waiter came and took their order, and they were left alone. She did like that about European restaurants. No one hovered. They wanted you to relax and take your time to enjoy the meal.

When she glanced back at Tate, she found he was studying her instead of their surroundings. She arched an eyebrow. "What?"

"Enjoying the view."

"Don't do that."

"I can't help it. You're a lovely woman. My opinion on that isn't something you've ever doubted, is it?"

"No." Chemistry had never been one of their problems. The great sex had probably helped float their relationship along much longer than it should have survived.

His shoulders rolled in a loose shrug. "Well, then."

Since there was no response she could give to that, she took a sip of her water. "I think I might wander through the Capitoline tomorrow. I always liked the sculptures and paintings there."

"Me too." He didn't mention that they'd explored the museum buildings together, admired the artwork several times during their yearlong courtship.

She glanced away so he couldn't see any memories that might reflect in her expression. "It opens at nine in the morning, so I thought I'd get an early start and push through some of the jetlag."

"Probably a good idea." He shifted in his seat. "I think we're only really expected for dinner every evening, so there's no reason for either of us to miss out on other sightseeing opportunities. We haven't been back since our year abroad."

Because he'd never been willing to take the time. It quivered on the tip of her tongue to point that out, but when she met his eyes, she saw that understanding reflected back at her. As he'd said that morning, he had a lot of regrets.

"I should have brought you back here. We both loved Italy. I should have made the time." The corners of his mouth tipped down. "I'm sorry, Karen."

"It's water under the bridge, Tate." And she needed to release the bitterness. It would only poison her in the end, and she wanted to move into a better future, not let the past drag her down. "I don't want to rub your nose in old mistakes."

"But can you forgive me for them?" His gaze was intent, sudden tension tightening the lines of his shoulders.

"I—" She blinked, the question catching her off-guard, and pain wrenched in her belly. "I don't know. I don't hate you for them. I don't even hate your father for being a domineering dick who turned my husband into Mini-Robert. But total forgiveness? With time, maybe I could. Last night, not using protection, could tie us all together genetically forever. I don't want to make a child some pawn in a little war between us."

"I would never do that." He leaned forward, tapping a finger against the table for emphasis.

"Robert would."

"I'm not him. No matter how close I came, I will never be him." His throat worked. "I don't work for him anymore. I won't be living near him anymore. The influence he has over my life just dropped down to nil. Don't forget that. I know I messed up, Karen. My life, your life, our marriage. I wish I could go back and change things, but I can't."

Sincerity radiated off him in waves, and for a moment, she saw the young man she'd fallen in love with in the first place. The one who looked her in the eye, listened to her, cared enough to put her needs first. Unsettled, she clenched shaking fingers under the table.

"So, where does that leave us? Future divorcees and possible future parents." She shook her head. "What a mess we've both made."

"Truer words, sweetheart, have never been spoken." He sat back as the waiter arrived with their food. "So, what do we do with this mess?"

"Muddle through as best we can, I guess. We won't know anything about consequences of last night until after the wedding, so I suggest we enjoy the time off work, enjoy Rome, enjoy our friends." She forked a bite of her pasta up and saluted him. "Right now, I'm just planning to enjoy lunch."

F reedom had never felt so sweet. His phone hadn't rung once in over twenty-four hours. He'd gotten confirmation that his resignation was delivered, sent emails on what to do with his caseload, and asked his assistant to pack up his office. Then he'd unplugged entirely. No email, no phones, no nothing. He was just sipping coffee outside the Capitoline Museum waiting for Karen to show up. It was bliss.

Of course, she didn't know he'd be waiting here for her, so his welcome was a bit suspect, but he'd figure out what to do when she arrived.

She'd said she might forgive him. Some day. He could work with that. He didn't expect a Get Out of Jail Free card for eight years of marital stupidity. He couldn't imagine that she'd suddenly believe he wouldn't take her for granted in the future. He had to start from scratch. No, worse than that. She'd be more willing to trust someone she'd just met. Him, she knew she couldn't put her faith in. He'd already failed her. Over and over again. He had a lot of ground to make up.

A bright flash of blonde hair caught his eye and he grinned. Karen, headed for the lengthy line to buy tickets at the museum entrance. He intercepted her before she got there. "You don't need to get in line."

Startling, she whirled to face him, a palm slapping over her chest. "Jesus, don't sneak up on people like that."

"Sorry." He rocked back on his heels. "Didn't mean to scare you."

Her green eyes narrowed. "What are you doing here?"

"The same thing you are, I imagine." He gave her his most charming smile, holding out a sheet of paper for her to look at. "And I was hoping you wouldn't mind company, so I decided to buy tickets online in a blatant attempt to bribe you."

Her mouth pursed in a way that said she was struggling not to smile. "Bribery is beneath you, Patton."

"Maybe, but I seem to have this extra ticket, and if you wanted to accept it as a small donation, you could bypass the massive line." He winked. "Think about it."

She wrinkled her nose, but stepped away from the snaking queue of people. "You're a pain in the ass, you know that, right?"

"Yes, but I have tickets." He set his hand on the small of her back and steered her toward the entrance. The heat of her supple flesh seeped through her cotton blouse, and he relished the opportunity to touch her. He'd missed having her in his bed last night, but a drunken sexcapade wasn't the way to win back a woman as prudent as Karen.

Her brow puckered. "I don't remember it being this crowded."

"We were here during the off-season." He tossed his coffee cup in the trash, showed the printed receipt for tickets to the attendant at the turnstiles, and then they were in. "The tourists have been unleashed."

She glanced over her shoulder at him. "Including us."

"Yep." He shortened his stride to match hers automatically.

They wandered through the many rooms in companionable silence, making the occasional quip or comment, but they were together and it wasn't strained or awkward. Tate called that a win.

The Capitoline Venus made him waggle his eyebrows, leaning down to whisper in Karen's ear. "I love that her left hand pretends to be all modest and yet we still get a full-frontal on her rack."

She coughed into her fist, clearly smothering a guffaw. "I love that you're retaining your inner middle-schooler. Do you still giggle when anyone says the word penis?"

"Certainly not." He brushed a palm down his shirtfront, pretending outrage, which made her grin, just as he'd hoped. "Let's see what's in the next room. Maybe one of the gruesome hunting paintings or that dying Gaul statue. More manly, less boobs."

He slipped his hands into his pockets and moved along, but not before he heard her snort of laughter.

Eventually, they came to the marble sculpture of Cupid and Psyche embracing in a kiss. Longing burned in his chest. Somehow it had escaped his mind that they'd be seeing this piece again. At twenty-one, he'd teased her into their first kiss in front of this statue. At thirty-three, he felt more uncertain and gauche than he ever had in his life, standing next to the only woman he'd ever wanted to spend his life with. Oh, to be carefree, cock-sure, and barely old enough to drink again. A bittersweet smile curled his lips.

"I can tell what you're thinking about."

He kept his gaze fixed on the white marble, framed by a window with blue sky beyond. "We went to a lot of museums that year. Somehow, I forgot about this piece being here."

"I didn't," she replied softly.

He glanced down at her. A little smile curved her mouth, and he was glad this at least was a good memory for her. The sunlight caught in her hair when she turned her head to meet his gaze. The moment spun into something intimate—this place had a shared history, a day that had redefined life as they'd known it. He reached up to tug on one of her shortened locks, the strands as lovely and golden as they'd ever been. God, he loved her. Her tongue flicked out to moisten her lips, and he had to kiss her.

"Something else for old time's sake." He tilted her chin up, gave her plenty of time to pull back, and then leaned forward to brush his mouth over hers. Once, twice. Their lips clung for long, sweet seconds. Brief, but perfect. His heart tripped against his ribs, and a fist of pure want gripped his insides. Her perfume teased his nose, and the fleeting slide of her breasts over his chest teased other parts of his anatomy.

He pulled back and found her eyes were closed, her mouth still pursed, and he kissed her again, lingering for an instant longer than was strictly acceptable in public, but he couldn't help himself. The lonely months without her made him starved for the taste of her, the feel of her curves against him. Breaking away, he dragged in a calming breath, wishing they were back in their hotel where he could get his hands on her in a much more satisfying way. He sucked his lower lip between his teeth, capturing the lingering essence of her taste.

She cleared her throat and turned to the next sculpture, leaving him no choice but to follow. She looked at the piece, but he doubted she really saw it. Her eyes seemed glazed and her fingers were white-knuckled on her purse strap. "Gio suspects something, you know. About us."

He blinked a few times, trying to get his brain to catch up with the conversational jump. "Ah...yeah, I noticed."

At dinner the night before, Karen had refused any wine, pleading a headache from overindulgence. She and Tate had shared a speaking glance. Of course, if she might be pregnant, she didn't want to continue drinking. Tate had stuck with water too, claiming the same reason as Karen. When he'd looked up, he'd found Giovanni studying them. Tate feared the Italian saw far more than he was comfortable with, but he'd given his friend a glare that would scorch paint and Gio had kept his mouth shut.

Yes, Gio suspected something. How much, Tate didn't really care to know.

Karen's mouth flattened. "Do you think he'll say anything to Valentina?"

"I don't know. I do know I'm holding him to his promise not to play matchmaker anymore." He took her hand, squeezing her fingers reassuringly. "Try not to worry about it. Like you said, we won't have any real news for a while. I can take care of Gio. Don't let him stress you out."

She stared down at their joined hands, then shook her head. "Tate, what are we doing?"

As if he was giving an honest answer to that question. The kiss had clearly freaked her out—something she couldn't blame on alcohol—and if he told her he wanted to shred the divorce papers and live happily ever after, she might actually run screaming. So he tugged her toward the next exhibit. "What are we doing? Enjoying Rome. Isn't that what you wanted?"

She slipped her hand free to scuttle ahead of him. He let her go and made no comment. After a few more rooms, a few quips about the art pieces, she cracked a smile and began to relax again.

This process would be two steps forward and one step back. He understood that and it was no more than he deserved. No doubt Karen had been far more frustrated by watching their marriage wither than he was by trying to resurrect it. But he had proximity to his advantage. And he had Rome, where all the memories they'd made were good. He'd be taking shameless advantage of that, reminding her that it wasn't all bad between them.

The foundation they'd laid for their relationship was solid—they could rebuild if they wanted.

CHAPTER FIVE

"**D**arling, this one would look fabulous on you! You must buy it." Valentina held up a skimpy lace teddy that was more see-through than not. It was in a rich shade of green that Karen had to admit would look great with her eyes and skin tone. Not that she was admitting that aloud.

She arched an eyebrow. "Focus, please. We're shopping for the naughty nights of your honeymoon, Ms. De Rossi, not my nonexistent sex life."

Lightning was going to strike her dead for that lie, and scenes from her first night in Rome flashed luridly through her mind. It had been three days since then, and except for that tiny, innocent little kiss at the museum, she'd kept her hands to herself. It was sad that she had to be proud of herself for her restraint at not jumping her almost-ex's bones. As Anne had pointed out, chemistry was a fickle little bitch.

"You're not dead. You'll need something like this again someday." With a great show of reluctance, Valentina hung the garment back on its rack.

The exclusive lingerie boutique catered to those with both expensive and prurient tastes. Which meant it was perfect for Valentina. So far, she had a leather bustier that made her breasts defy gravity and logic, a pink riding crop, and something made out of silk that Karen wasn't sure she wanted any details about. She wasn't staid or prudish—Tate had never lacked for inventiveness nor she a willingness to give almost anything a try—but there were a few things that didn't rev her engine. Everyone was entitled to her own preferences in the bedroom.

Valentina tapped a manicured finger against her cheek. "What do you think? The red corset and matching thong, the translucent cream negligee, or the French maid costume?"

Tipping her head to the side to consider her friend's options, Karen replied, "Get all three, but go for the cream negligee on your wedding night. Keep it classic."

"An excellent point." Turning to the saleswoman, Valentina flashed a charming smile, spoke in rapid Italian and within ten minutes they were on their way again. Valentina looped her arm through Karen's as they walked along the cobblestone pedestrian zone that held many of the other woman's favorite shops. "Thank you for coming with me today. My mother would surely have enjoyed that shop far more than I want to know about. If she'd bought a whip for my father, I might have died."

"I'm happy to provide an escort." Karen chuckled. "Your family seems to think you'll get lost if they let you wander off on your own."

"They think because they are not often in *Roma*, I must be lost here too." A musical laugh trickled out of Valentina. "I've been trying to convince them for many years that I'm not a small-town girl anymore, but they'll never believe it."

"Family," Karen agreed in a long-suffering tone. She glanced at her watch. "We need to make sure we're on time to the fitting for your gown."

"You will love my dress!" A little skipping step almost tripped both women. "It is perfect. *Un bel vestito*."

Holding on to keep them upright, Karen shook her head at the exuberance. "I can't wait to see it."

And so the afternoon went, Karen getting swept along in the force of nature that was Valentina. She insisted on two new bathing suits for the honeymoon in Bora Bora, earrings to match each one, a new pair of sunglasses, three slinky wrap dresses for the beach and pretty sandals. Karen didn't even mention price tags—she knew Gio would be happy to buy his bride an entire wardrobe if that kept the wedding on track. And they could afford it, so why rain on the parade?

To appease her friend, Karen picked up a few inexpensive souvenirs. Funky handkerchiefs that would amuse her brother, a silk tie in her dad's favorite color. A bracelet for her mother, unique necklaces for Anne, Meg, and Julie, and a pretty pair of peridot earrings for herself that would go perfectly with the dress she'd brought for the wedding. Because of the short notice, Valentina and Gio had insisted on no gifts from any guests, so Karen didn't have to worry about sneaking in shopping for that.

She was ready to collapse when the cab dropped her off at her hotel. Valentina could shop like nobody's business. But Karen only had time to drop off her purchases, catch a quick shower, and throw on a dress before she had to make a dash for dinner. Valentina's grandmother was old school enough to believe in wearing nice clothing for the evening meal. Shorts were verboten and jeans would send the old lady into a swoon.

After getting to her room, Karen dumped her bags on the bed and went to hose off in the bathroom. Of course, the moment she hopped out of the tub, her cell phone rang. She ran to her purse, grabbed her cell, and found it was someone using Skype to call her.

She turned on the speakerphone. "Hello?"

"Hey, hon. It's Julie."

"Hi!" Karen set the phone on the bathroom counter and began applying makeup. "I'm getting ready for dinner, so...multitasking."

"Right, it's afternoon there." Her friend cleared her throat. "Um. How's Rome?"

The hesitant tone let Karen draw the obvious conclusion. "Anne talked to you."

"She said you said it was okay, but that we weren't to mention it. So I'm calling to check in and not mentioning...things." Julie took an audible breath. "So. How's Rome?"

Karen swept blush across her cheekbones, considering her answer. Might as well confess her stupidity—her friends would drag every detail out when she got home anyway. At least she didn't have to look them in the eye this way. "I let him kiss me. In front of the Cupid statue where we kissed the first time."

There was a long pause. "Was it good?"

Karen jammed a hand down on her hip and glared at the phone. "See? This is why I shouldn't be talking to you. You're the instigator in the group! You always egged us on as kids just to see what would happen."

"So it was good." Satisfaction oozed through Julie's voice, and she didn't protest the instigator label for an instant. "There's nothing wrong with a really good kiss. A girl needs those from time to time."

Wrinkling her nose, Karen sighed. "Yeah, it was good."

"Is he trying to get you back or something?"

She finished applying her make-up and then carried the cell into her bedroom and laid it on the nightstand. "He hasn't said anything like that. The drunk sex was...drunk sex. The kiss was like hearing someone sing *Memories* in my ear while twelve years ago flashed before my eyes."

Julie spoke softly, "Do you want him to try to get you back?"

"No, of course not," Karen snapped. Her heart tripped and she ignored it. She wouldn't even let herself consider something so insane, so emotionally suicidal. She would not.

"That protest was a little too fast and a little too loud to be believable, hon."

"I just...we broke up...I had very good reasons for dumping his ass...but everything is just so confused. We're here again. In Rome." She rubbed her forehead. "And he quit his job."

"What?" Julie screeched the word so loudly the receiver squealed. "Wait, wait, wait. Wait. Workaholic Tate Patton quit his job. I heard that right?"

"He's going to start his own law firm, he says." Karen still wasn't sure how she felt about that. Resentment and the kind of stinging ache you got when you pressed on a bruise. "Not in Palo Alto. He's moving away."

"Where to?" Suspicion colored the other woman's tone.

"He's not sure yet."

"I'd bet he's seriously considering Half Moon Bay."

"Julie," she groaned.

"He's gonna try to get you back," Julie insisted. "He's realized he was an enormous idiot and a complete horse's ass and you were the best thing that ever happened to him. Make sure he grovels appropriately before you even consider it."

"Julie!"

"I'm just saying. You deserve begging. And presents. And really toe-curling sex. Like, the best you've ever had."

Karen huffed out a breath. "Did you make Lukas beg when he stomped all over your heart?"

"He apologized, but he was an idiot for a couple of weeks, not the better part of a decade. Plus, we weren't married. Time and commitment level counts." Complete conviction rang in her friend's voice. "I mean, if you want him back, go for it. Just make sure you torture him enough that he's never that dumb again. Or you can just use him as a sex toy while you're there and forget about any kind of reconciliation. Have fun."

"Instigator!"

"Only because I love you." Julie made an exaggerated kissing noise. "Go to dinner. And, remember, Tate owes you the best sex of your life, whether you take him back or not. Make him pay up."

"Goodbye, insane woman." Karen stabbed the screen to cut the call.

After shoving her feet into strappy, high-heeled sandals, she grabbed her purse and hustled out the door. Forget walking, she was going to need a taxi to get to Valentina's on time.

When she entered the apartment, the place was already crowded. More family members seemed to spill in every day. Gio's was local, so they didn't feel the need to be there every second of the day, but they joined in on the boisterous dinners.

Of course, she was pushed into the chair next to Tate. Of course. It was no longer weird, just a déjà vu feeling of the past coming back to haunt her. She tried to ignore the press of his muscular thigh against hers, the slide of his broad shoulder as it brushed her arm—as she'd done every other evening. It was a futile effort. Her body reacted to his nearness, her breasts growing heavy, her sex aching with a need that wouldn't quit. Even with the heady aroma of Italian food floating in the air, she could swear she smelled his musky cologne.

He turned to her. "How was your day?"

His tone was polite, but something in his gaze made her wary. "Fine.

Valentina shopped until I dropped."

"Mmm. She mentioned a trip to a naughty lingerie and toy shop." His eyes widened innocently. "Did you buy anything?"

The green teddy flashed through her mind, and heat burned her cheeks. "No, I didn't."

A warm voice rumbled in her ear as he leaned close. "Then why are you blushing?"

Her tongue stuck to the roof of her mouth. He'd turned just enough that he was plastered against her from knee to shoulder and a hot wave of utter want shook her. Her nipples went taut, her thighs quivering. This was crazy, but her brain and her body were at war because she had to clench her fingers to stop from touching him. Julie's words about using him as a sex toy came back in a rush. There was no way Karen could do that. Not if she wanted to avoid a one-way ticket back to the emotional quagmire she'd pried herself out of when she left him. Every rational scrap of her soul told her to ignore the innuendo in his question, but she'd been fighting her desire for him since she'd woken up in his bed with a massive hangover. Which side would win?

She resolutely picked up her fork and speared a mushroom, refusing to look at him, refusing to acknowledge that using him for sex was far too tempting an idea. Curse Julie and her instigating ways.

"No answer, hmm?" His breath brushed over her neck and she shivered. "Did you know your nipples are hard, Karen?"

Closing her eyes, she swallowed. Thank God they were speaking softly enough that no one would hear them over the raucous dinner party. "A slight chill, that's all."

Sweet Baby Jesus, a *chill?* That was the best she had to fend him off? She was burning up, flames licking over her flesh. His scent filled her nostrils—hot, masculine, and all Tate. He overwhelmed every sense, and another shiver ran through her.

"Mmm, are you sure? I can also see your pulse pounding. Right here." One fingertip stroked across the base of her throat. "Why is your heart racing, Karen?"

As if she could answer that question. But Tate was a lawyer, and he hadn't risen to the top of his profession by giving up at the first challenge. Nope, he was nothing if not persistent. She'd just forgotten what it felt like to be the focus of all his intensity. Intoxicating, addicting, thrilling.

"I think..." He paused as if considering the situation. "I think you're turned on right now. Do you have any idea what that does to me?"

"What?" The word was out of her mouth before she could stop it.

He gave no verbal reply, just took her hand and casually slipped it into his lap under the table. His breath hissed in when she shaped her palm and fingers around the thick ridge of his erection. Just because she could, because maybe a little torture was exactly what he deserved, she stroked him through his slacks for a few seconds. Impossibly, he grew harder, his shaft pulsing against her hand.

"Karen." An edge of pleading filled his deep voice, and she liked that. She liked it far more than she should.

She pulled her arm away before anyone noticed what they were up to. "Eat your dinner, Patton."

A pained chuckle came from him, but he eased out of her personal space. "You're a sadist, love."

Love. Her heart twinged at that moniker. She lifted her chin. "You seem to like it. Maybe I should have been meaner during our marriage."

Some unnamable emotion flashed through his gaze, but he just arched a challenging eyebrow. "Are you going to be mean to me later?"

"Maybe. If I feel like it." She pursed her lips and decided torturing him might be a lot more fun than she'd ever imagined. Something dark and naughty twisted inside her. "Eat your dinner. You might need to keep up your strength tonight. Then again, you might not."

A giddy sense of power flooded her, combining with the unfulfilled lust that sang through her body. She could have him if she wanted him, make him beg for her. Or not. It had been a very long time since she'd felt anything but inept, hopeless, and defenseless. But this. This was how she wanted to feel. Sensual, powerful, womanly. She glanced at Tate from the corner of her eyes. He fidgeted—something he never did—and kept sneaking looks at her. Good, let him stew a little.

And maybe some seasoning to add to that stew... "So how do you feel about being tied up?"

His big body went rigid, his eyes sliding closed. "Yes, please."

Having him totally at her mercy—the thought was enough to give her hot flashes. She brushed invisible crumbs off her skirt. "Hmm. I'll think about it."

"So will I," he whispered.

"Good." She was going to do it. Take all the pleasure he had to give and then some. She was going to have a wildly irresponsible foreign affair with her ex. Maybe that was all it should have been when they'd met in college. She remembered how scared she'd been when she thought he wouldn't want to continue their relationship after they returned to the US.

A sigh slipped out of her, and she shook her head. No. She couldn't regret the last decade. She'd loved him desperately, and even knowing how it would end, she couldn't dismiss the happiness of her younger self. But she was older and wiser now, and she knew she didn't want to dive back into a relationship with him. She just wanted to take advantage of what had never gone wrong for them—wildly explosive attraction.

She'd never had frivolous, meaningless sex before, but it was sounding better and better by the second. Exactly what a foreign affair should be.

They left the apartment together after dinner, and damn if Tate hadn't had a semi the whole time they'd been there. Sure, he and Karen had tried the tied-up thing before, but Jesus, when was the last time she'd wanted him enough to be the aggressor? The sex had always been good, even when their relationship was at its worst, but he had a feeling tonight might make his head explode. If she decided to go through with it. The uncertainty, the teasing, just made his anticipation burn hotter. He was so desperate for her, he'd get down on his knees and beg if that would please her.

And that might be exactly what she had in mind.

His erection throbbed painfully, chafing against his fly. His gaze glued to her rounded ass as she preceded him down the stairs.

They reached the ground level and she turned her head to glance back at him. Her smirk told him he'd been caught staring.

"We need condoms."

Thank you, God. He swallowed. "I bought some. They're back in my hotel room."

Her eyes narrowed. "Oh, really. You were counting on this, huh?"

Cautiously, he replied, "I was hopeful, and I am careful. When sober."

A single brow arched and then she spun for the door. "Well, then. We shouldn't let them go to waste, should we? I hope you bought a lot."

Yeah, because that was going to make his boner settle down for the walk back to the hotel. "I can get more if it's not enough."

"We'll see."

He tried to ignore the discomfort of his hard-on as he strode beside her through the *Trastevere rione*, where the cobblestone streets were lined with parked cars. Old buildings rose four to five stories above them, painted in earthy tones of beige and cream and terra cotta, some covered in ivy. How many times had they walked this district together? Talking, laughing, discovering Rome and each other. He slid his hand into hers like it was the most natural thing in the world, and she didn't pull away. He let his thumb swirl around the inside of her palm, where he knew she was most sensitive, reminding them both of what was to come. When he glanced at her, he saw her nipples clearly outlined by her top. He wanted to suck them.

Holding the door to the hotel open, he waved her inside. She slipped in and made sure to let her breasts slide across his chest as she passed. Yeah, that was sweet. And a little mean. He liked the contrast. His erection stirred to life again, not that it had gone down entirely during their walk, but the bodily contact made what blood remained in his brain flow south.

They bypassed the slow, tiny elevator and climbed the stairs. He got another view of her backside, only now it was right at his eye level. It was all he could do not to drool. His hands shook with the need to stroke over her soft, bared curves.

When they reached their floor, he dug out his room keycard. The hallway was deserted, so their footsteps echoed unnaturally. Here it was. The moment of truth. Would she follow through on the teasing, or change her mind? Sobriety lent a much different perspective.

She stopped by his door, and he quickly unlocked it and held it open for her. This time, she didn't brush against him. She lifted one hand and boldly ran a fingertip around his nipple. He jerked, the air seizing in his lungs. Fire licked through his veins, and his shaft went diamond hard in under three seconds. "Karen..."

"How many neckties did you bring with you?" She pinched his nipple, twisting slowly.

He swallowed, gripping the doorknob so tight it squeaked. "Four."

"Good." She dropped her hand, grazing her knuckles across his fly as she stepped into his room.

He sucked in a breath, shuddering with a lust so intense it almost drove him to his knees. It took him a moment to muster enough control to follow her in and close and lock the door behind him.

"Hmm." Karen set her hands on her hips and stared at the bed. "The knobs on the top of the headboard look sturdy enough, don't you think?"

They did. "Yes."

She nodded in satisfaction, and then started stripping while he watched. The sight of her creamy skin was breathtaking. Her curves had filled out in the twelve years since they'd met, and she was even more beautiful now than she had been then. Her dress fell away, leaving her in sapphire blue underwear. She was a goddess, skin like a moonbeam, hair like sunshine. Her breasts threatened to spill from her bra when she bent forward to slip off her panties.

And then she was naked and Tate could have died a happy man.

She gave him an amused glance. "Are you going to get me the ties and take your clothes off, or just stand there?"

"I'm enjoying the view. Give me a moment." He moved his gaze over her, pausing at all his favorite places. Her nipples peaked and her breathing hitched. A flush pinkened her skin, and he loved seeing the evidence of her desire. It only whetted his own.

"Nope, I don't want to wait." She placed a palm against the lower swell of her belly, gliding down into the pale curls at the juncture of her thighs. Her fingertips dipped in, her hips pressing toward the touch.

Tate groaned, utter need throbbing through him. "Point taken."

He went to the closet where he'd draped his ties over a hanger and slipped free the three there, then unwound the one at his throat. After he handed them all to Karen, he shucked his shoes and clothes in short order. He fetched the small box of condoms he'd purchased and set it on the nightstand.

She knotted the ties together in sets of two, and fastened the end of one set around the base of the thick knob on his headboard. She tossed the other set to him and he did the same on his side of the bed.

"Lay down."

A bead of moisture slipped down his shaft, and a quiver passed through his body. He craved her so badly he wanted to pounce, roll her under him and take her hard and fast. It took every ounce of his self-discipline to do as she asked. He stretched out on the mattress, holding his arms wide so she could bind his wrists. Reflexively, he tugged at the ties and found he was truly trapped. His heart tripped against his ribs, and his excitement and anticipation ratcheted up by the moment.

A sexy little smile curved her lips, and the devious twinkle in her green gaze should have made him wary, but didn't. He was up for whatever she had in store.

She got on her knees beside him and looked him over as thoroughly as he'd done for her. Then she frowned and poked an index finger into his chest. "This doesn't mean we're getting back together."

He winced a little, but then shrugged. "I don't think I ever asked you for that."

Now it was her turn to wince. "Good, then we're agreed. Just a short affair while we're in Rome."

He grunted in reply rather than lie. Time for some distraction. He eyed her taut nipples. "I want to suck you. If you'd bend forward just a bit, I could..."

Her gaze darkened and a deep breath made those luscious breasts rise. "Maybe. If I feel like it. Right now, I get to decide what we do or don't do."

"I do seem to be at your mercy." He wiggled his bound wrists. "Whatever will you do with me?"

The smile that flashed across her face was brilliant. She sat back on her heels and looked at him like he was a chocolate truffle in her favorite candy store. She reached out a single finger and drew random patterns on his chest, circled his nipples, tickled his side until he squirmed, traced his hipbone, slipped down his leg to his foot. Then she started on the other side and worked her way back up. She touched him everywhere except where he craved it most. He was going to die before she was done with him.

"Karen, please. Please."

"Please, what?" After leaning forward, she let a hot breath rush over his erection.

A hoarse sound dragged from his throat and he arched toward her mouth, but she straightened, the witch. Her brows arched innocently while he writhed in frustration, jerking at the bindings.

"Suck me. Ride me hard. Let me come. Please." His voice was more demanding than pleading, but he couldn't help himself.

"Suck you, huh?"

Sweat beaded on his skin, and he couldn't stop moving, shifting against the sheets, his body pulsing with lust. "Yes."

"Okay." A devilish grin formed on her lips, then she dipped down to suck his nipple into her mouth.

A growl was the only sound he could make, his body bowing off the bed. The ties snapped taut, and he gripped the silk above the knots in an effort to hold on to his sanity when she switched to the other nipple. Her slender fingers drifted down to encircle his shaft and he choked on a breath. She stroked him, her thumb rolling over the bulbous crest.

Yes. God, yes. He gasped, "More."

Her tongue trailed down the centerline of his chest, his abs, and then—*thank you, Jesus*—she licked his shaft from base to crown. Her hot, wet mouth closed over him and he moaned. His hips bucked, trying to push himself deeper. She chuckled and the vibration shivered down the length of his erection and he almost came then and there.

But she backed off, letting him slip free of her lips.

"Fuck," he groaned. His eyes closed, jaw clenched, and a muscle ticked in his cheek.

"Aw, poor baby." Sharp teeth nipped at the edge of his navel, and he jerked in shock.

His eyes flew open, and there was a gloating expression on her face. Her palms pressed to his chest and she brushed her lips over his. How had he not asked her to kiss him yet? The flavor of her filled his mouth—tart and sweet and so uniquely Karen. Their tongues dueled for control of the contact, their breathing ragged.

"Untie me, Karen. I want to touch you."

"Mmm." Her hand went down to tease his shaft and cup the soft sac beneath. "Are you sure you want to be let loose?"

"No. Yes. No." There was a certain eroticism to the helplessness, and that made him want even more. Her. This. Now. "I have to slide inside you. I need to be inside you. Please, sweetheart."

She slipped off the bed, walking around the end of it. After pausing to tickle his feet, she snagged a condom from the nightstand.

"Thank God."

Laughing at him, she unwrapped the protection and covered him with it. He was so turned on, even that small touch was enough to make his breath catch. She moved to straddle his waist. The first brush of her wet sex against his and his hips shoved upward, trying to bury himself in her.

"Ah, ah, ah." She shimmied upward so he couldn't penetrate her, but that left her breasts within reach of his mouth. He turned his head and captured one stiff peak, suckling hard. She gasped his name, her fingers digging into his shoulders. He felt little shivers ripple through her, heard the panting sound of her breath, felt the heat of her skin as sweat glued their flesh together.

He released her nipple, and she shoved her hips back to take him deep. They both moaned when he was fully seated within her slick, silky passage. She bit her lower lip, then lifted and lowered herself on him. With each of her downward plunges, he pushed up, filling her completely. The tight squeeze of her channel was incredible, perfect.

"You feel so good."

She winked. "You're not so bad yourself."

She set a leisurely pace that was far, far too slow for him. He yanked at the ties, trying to push for greater speed, knowing there was nothing in the world more gorgeous than Karen's face when she shattered. He wanted to watch her when she came for him.

"Kiss me again," he whispered.

She leaned in to give him what he asked for. The tart-sweet taste of her was an aphrodisiac. He angled his hips, rolling his pelvis in a way he knew would drive her crazy. She whimpered into his mouth, and he sucked on her tongue, bit her lip. Suddenly her movements weren't slow, but hard and fast and exactly what he wanted.

Breaking her mouth away from his, she threw her head back and let out a sob as she hit climax. He felt the flex and release of her inner muscles, and it was more than enough to make him explode. He jetted inside her, and a euphoric rush hit him. Still he never took his gaze from her expression, loving the way her eyes lost focus, and the bliss he felt reflected back from her green, green eyes.

She collapsed forward on to his chest, both of them gasping for breath, coated in sweat, and shaking in the aftermath. A sigh heaved out of him, and after long moments had passed his heart finally stopped racing. His shoulders burned from where the ties were stretched taut, and the discomfort of his position began to bring him back to reality.

"Okay, untie me, please. My arms are starting to cramp and I can't feel my fingers."

"Oh, sorry!" She sat up, slipped off of him and worked at the knots. Concern shone on her face. "How on earth did these get so tight?"

"I pulled at them." He grinned. "Couldn't help it. You make me wild."

She blushed but managed a demure shrug. "It's a gift, what can I say?"

The ties slipped free, and she rubbed his arms and hands for him. He closed his eyes and let himself savor the moment, the attention and caring. He'd missed this, missed everything about being with her. After a few minutes, she lay next to him on the bed and sighed, the sound so thoroughly satisfied it made him smile.

He rose from the bed. "I'll be right back."

"Mmkay." Her tone was soft and hazy, and she didn't so much as twitch.

A quick trip and he'd cleaned up, then headed back, afraid if he left her alone too long she might decide to bail for the night. He had other plans. When he returned, he found her exactly where she had been, eyes shut, bonelessly relaxed on the mattress. He had to admit to a little bit of pride at having pleased her so well.

But there was always room for improvement.

The sight of her naked form had predictable effects on his body, and he donned another condom. Then he crawled up the mattress, nudging her legs apart until he settled between them.

Her eyes flared wide, a surprised laugh spilling from her lips. "Again?"

"Oh, yeah." And then he thrust in deep and proved it.

CHAPTER SIX

T ate woke up with the most amazing sense of peace that he'd ever felt in his entire life. A smile curved his lips before he even opened his eyes. Karen's head rested on his shoulder, her body pressed to his side. God, yes. This was what he wanted, needed, craved every morning for the rest of his days.

Unfortunately, he also needed to pee. He eased to the right, and Karen murmured in her sleep and rolled away from him, curling onto her side. Rising quickly, he went and took care of business, then brushed his teeth. It tasted like something had died in his mouth overnight, so toothpaste was a definite must.

Karen was yawning and rubbing her eyes when he got back. After walking over, he bent down to brace his hands on either side of her shoulders and kissed her. "Morning."

"Hey." She patted his jaw and yawned again. "What time is it?"

He dropped to the mattress beside her, then glanced at the clock. "About 8:30."

"I should get up." Stretching against the sheets, she let out little squeaky noises that made him laugh.

But his mirth faded when she really did get up and reach for her dress.

"Wait, wait. Not yet." He hauled her back so she sprawled across his chest, claiming her mouth in a deep, thorough kiss. All thought trickled out of his brain as his shaft went rigid. His heart began to pound, thrumming against his eardrums. His senses filled with her—taste, touch, scent—soft and so sweet he ached.

"Shouldn't you get that?" she asked against his lips.

Air shuddered into his lungs. "Hmm? What?"

Breathy laughter escaped her. "Your phone, Mr. Patton. It's ringing."

"Ignore it." He tried to capture her mouth again, but she evaded him.

"Isn't that your sister's ring tone?"

It was. He muttered, "Crap."

She chuckled, popping a quick kiss on his lips. "Later, Tate."

She dressed and disappeared like so much smoke, slipping through his fingers. He didn't like it, wanted her to stay forever, but he couldn't expect that. Yet. He'd catch up with her in a little while. Last night had only made him more determined than ever to overcome their problems.

The phone had stopped ringing, but he pulled on a pair of boxers, grabbed his cell and called his sister back.

She picked up within seconds. "Hey, bro! I was just about to leave you a message."

"Luckily, I saved you the effort." He flopped onto the mattress and stuffed a pillow under his head. "What's up, kid?"

"You realize I'm over thirty years old, right?"

He shrugged even though she couldn't see it. "You'll always be my kid sister. Deal with it."

"Says the guy who ran away from home," she retorted.

A direct hit. He tried not to flinch. "Was there something you actually wanted?"

She made a little noise. "Well, I was staying with Mom and Dad for a few days while I met with some people from the gallery to prep for my show."

Anytime that Laurel was within ten miles of his parents, there was bound to be fireworks. Or nuclear warfare. "Sounds like fun."

"So dry, so witty."

He bit back a laugh and arched his eyebrows. "There was a point to this international phone call, I'm sure of it."

"I'm house-sitting for you," she replied loftily.

"Oh?" Now he didn't bother to smother the chuckle. "I need a house-sitter?"

"Yes, because otherwise your sister is going to murder your father." Her voice turned grim. "He's been ranting for days because his son jumped ship and some of his clients want to jump with him. Some of his lawyers too."

That brought Tate upright. "What?"

It was her turn to chuckle. "You haven't checked your email, have you?"

"No, I unplugged. I'm on vacation." His tone was more defensive than he liked, but he'd been a workaholic for a lot of years. It would be a hard habit to break, but he'd do it if it killed him. He resisted the urge to login now and verify what his sister said. He had an automated away message up—that would have to do. He was offline until he got back to the States, period.

"Wow, you really have turned over a new leaf." Laurel sounded equal parts shocked and pleased. "I'm so proud of you. Really."

Because he didn't know how to react to praise anymore, since he'd rarely gotten any from his father and less and less from his wife as the years had worn on, he went back to the original topic. "So, you figure I owe you for pissing off Dad and you're taking your payment by using my house as your personal bed and breakfast?"

"It's old enough and pretty enough to be a B&B," she enthused. "And I'm doing you a favor by house-sitting while you're overseas. So thieves won't think your home is easy pickings. You're welcome."

Her utter lack of shame made him shake his head. She'd been that way since the day she was born. He rolled his eyes. "Uh-huh. Make sure you disarm the security system. You have your own code. And do not get paint all over my house. Work in the garage."

She huffed. "I wasn't planning to work while I was in town."

"I know you better than that," he said drily. "Keep your paints outside the house, Laurel. Anything you mess up, you'll pay to fix."

He could all but see her wrinkling her nose. "Fine, I'll stick to the garage."

"There you go."

She hesitated. "Dad says you're trying to get Karen back. He framed it in ruder terms than that, but...is he right?"

Considering the terms their father had used with Tate, he had no doubt what was said wasn't worth repeating. So he didn't comment on that and just answered the question. "Yes. If she'll have me."

"I hope she does," Laurel replied quietly. "You know you'll never find anyone who suits you better. She's the best there is."

Scooting back against the headboard, he nodded. "I know."

In a far more chipper tone, his sister said, "Plus, sexy librarian. I told you that the day I met her."

He snorted. "I remember."

"And I was right."

That day, that week when Karen had first been thrust into the chaos of his family—was burned pretty clearly in his memory. It had been the tipping point for whether or not he'd ask her to marry him. Could she put up with the insanity of being a Patton? Would she want to? She'd said she could handle it, and he'd promised not to turn into his father. They'd both been wrong. Or he had been first, and since he'd reneged on their agreement, she'd had no reason to stick around.

"She might not take me back."

His sister gave a sympathetic hum. "You did go all Dad on her. And she's not emotionally constipated and morally bankrupt like Mom, so she's not the type to put up with that forever."

"Our parents aren't evil, Laurel." As the sometimes-flaky artist of the family, Laurel had absolutely never seen eye to eye with their image-conscious, controlled and controlling parents. On any issue. Ever. He'd been the go-between in so many fights growing up, persuading both sides to come to compromises—what other career could he have gone for than a lawyer?

"No, they're not evil," she agreed, much to his surprise. Laurel had grown up, matured enough to see the shades of gray in their family dynamic. Tate wondered when that had happened, and knew he'd missed it as he had so many other things in the years he'd worked for his dad. Laurel sighed. "And we turned out okay, but they never knew how to deal with children who didn't turn out like them."

True. He'd done his best to shield her, to convince his parents to give her room to be herself, but it had never been enough. "I'm sorry they gave you a hard time. I should have done more to—"

"No, you shouldn't have." She cut him off, turning severe. "You did everything you could to protect me from their look-the-other-way-during-little-affairs lifestyle. No one could protect me from their socialite expectations or their disappointment when I couldn't meet them. The only difference between us is that you could meet those expectations—at least for a while—and I never could. But I'd rather deal with their disappointment than with my own if I turned into them."

A knife of pain stabbed into his chest. That certainly drove the point home, didn't it? "Welcome to my life right now."

She made a regretful sound. "I'm sorry. That's not what I meant."

"It's still true."

"You were always a good brother and a much better son than Robert and Francesca deserved, even if you weren't the best husband."

He shook his head. "It's easy to be a good brother when you haven't lived in the same time zone as me since you were eighteen and left for college."

"Well, that might be changing. The West Coast has been calling my name lately."

"Really?" He wouldn't mind seeing her more often. Laurel could be crazy-making, but she was also a breath of fresh air in the otherwise stifled Patton clan. Though sometimes that air came at hurricane-force speeds.

"Yes, really. Now, can we get back to my point about your good/bad ratio?" He heard a rustling noise as his sister shifted the phone. "Look, you never cheated on Karen, never deliberately hurt her. That doesn't excuse you, but you're not a terrible person. I know you, and you're all coulda-shoulda-woulda in your head like you're the biggest dickhead of all time. Well, you're not. You're the road-to-hell-is-paved-with-good-intentions guy. Try not to beat yourself up too hard. You do deserve to be happy."

Another direct hit. He had been kicking his own ass a lot. He deserved the beating, but he didn't necessarily deserve to be miserable. Then again, wasn't that what he'd been lately? Utterly miserable. He wanted to be happy. He wanted Karen to be happy too. "Thanks, sis.

I needed to hear that."

"She may not be able to forgive you, but don't make that mean you can't forgive yourself."

He winced. "That's harder."

"I know, but it's also important," Laurel insisted. "You guys grew apart and you need to grow back together. If you can't, that doesn't mean you should stop growing as a person. For years, you've been clipping yourself down like one of the perfectly manicured topiaries in Mom and Dad's garden. Go a little wild."

His mind flashed to everything he and Karen had done to each other since they came to Italy. "I'm working on it."

"Good."

He grinned. "You're pretty smart for a baby sister, you know."

"Yep, I know."

The smugness oozing out of those words just couldn't go unanswered. He quipped, "Must be from all those rough years as a starving artist."

Which she'd never experienced. Even while struggling to establish herself, she'd had a trust fund to keep her afloat.

She laughed. "Shut up!"

Swinging his feet over the edge of the bed, he prepared to get up and get ready for the day. "Thanks for calling. Enjoy the parental break in my house. There's no food in the fridge though."

"I'll pick up some groceries." Her sigh was long-suffering, as if she couldn't believe he wasn't prepared to feed her at any moment, whether he was on a different continent or not. "Good luck with Karen. Tell her I said hi. Have fun on your first vacation in over a decade. Enjoy Gio and Valentina's wedding."

"I will." Especially if Karen was there.

"Oh, and I dyed the tips of my hair purple."

Of course. Laurel was rarely without some portion of her dark locks being an electrifying shade. "Any new piercings or tattoos?"

"Still just the nose, navel and tragus. You know I don't do tats."

Mostly because she was a gigantic wimp about pain. A piercing was quick, a tattoo meant she'd have to sit there and take it. Possibly for multiple hours over several sessions. Not going to happen. Tate had had to hold her hand while she cried every time she'd needed booster shots as a child. He didn't tease her about it though. They all had their fears. "Whatever makes you happy, kid."

She chuckled. "Love you."

"Love you too." He moved to hang up and then stopped. "Will you still be there when I get back? How long are you in town?"

He could picture her face scrunched up as she tried to remember actual details about anything other than art. "Um...your return flight is on Wednesday?"

"Yes." He blinked. "Do I want to know how you know that?"

"I have your assistant's number." She blew a raspberry through the phone. "And, yes, I should still be here. I'll want to hear all about it. Unless there's sexy parts. Those you can filter down to PG level. You are my brother, after all."

"Yes, because I'm still traumatized by having to explain to you what condoms were." God knew their parents weren't having the sex talk with them. Tate had learned the gory details in health class—he'd just had the misfortune of being the oldest. "No thirteen-year-old boy should have to do such a thing for his eleven-year-old sister."

"I'm sure you can hug it out with your therapist," she drawled.

He laughed outright at that. Talking to Laurel always lightened his heart a little. Even when he wanted to strangle her. "See you next week."

"Later!" The line clicked as she cut the call.

Laurel had given him a lot to think about, but his goal was unchanged. He still wanted Karen—in his life and in his bed. He wanted her forgiveness, and no matter what his sister said, he wasn't entirely sure he could forgive himself for making such a shambles of his marriage without Karen's absolution.

But even if she didn't take him back, he was never going to work for his father again. The very thought made his stomach clench. No. Hell no. He was so done with that. Though if Laurel was right, his new practice was off to a good start. He'd be severely limiting his client list, but he wouldn't mind starting that list with those who'd been happy with his work before.

That was a concern for when he landed in the States. He was not checking email, and his clients didn't have his personal number, so he'd get messages from his assistant when he returned. *Former* assistant. Though with any luck, she was one of the people who wanted to follow him to his new firm. Good assistants were worth their weight in gold.

For now, he needed to get this reconciliation on track. Shower, dress, and see what Karen was up to. He hoped she was open to having company.

T ime for some touristing.

Karen hummed as she got ready for the day. She felt relaxed and mellow—telltale signs of really good sex—and she refused to experience even an ounce of guilt over it. There was no crime in getting laid, especially by someone who knew exactly what he was doing. And Tate did. That didn't make it anything other than really good sex. She ignored the niggle of conscience in the back of her mind, the tiny part of her that recognized her own lie. No. No guilt, no worrying, no repercussions, no emotional involvement. Just a straight-up shagfest.

After slathering on some sunblock, she stepped into a pair of sandals she could walk in for miles with no problem, and slung a small crossbody bag over her shoulder. All set.

She opened her door and fell back with a gasp. Tate leaned casually against the opposite wall, arms folded, ankles crossed. His eyes crinkled with amusement at her reaction, but he said nothing.

She frowned. "You're making a habit of scaring me, Patton. It's annoying."

His eyebrows winged upward. "I'll keep that in mind."

"How's Laurel?" She strove for a calm voice and a neutral topic, stomping down on the little flutter in her heart. She did not flutter for Tate Patton. Not anymore.

Dipping a shoulder, he shrugged. "She was staying with the parents while doing some prep work for her art show. She called to let me know she gave up on dealing with them and is house-sitting for me. To make sure all the unsavory elements in chichi Palo Alto don't decide to break in."

"Good of her." She grinned at his sister's characteristic audacity.

"She thought so." One side of his mouth tipped up. "She said to say hello. And she dyed her hair purple."

"Ha." After moving into the hallway, Karen let her door swing shut behind her. "I still remember your mom freaking out about Laurel's blue-streaked hair the first time I met your family."

"Part of the fun of coloring it, I'm sure. Also no doubt the reason for her recent dye job, since she was visiting the parental units."

"True." Karen smirked. "I have to admit, I always loved the way your mother's eyes bulged with outrage every time Laurel went a different shade."

"Me too." He winked in return. "So, where are you headed?"

She hesitated. Should she tell him? Invite him along? This was the problem with having sex with an ex when she was going to be in forced proximity with him for several days. There was no sexing it up and then walking away. Nope. Here he was. And just looking at him was sending tendrils of warmth unfurling inside her. He was gorgeous—all broad shoulders, lean muscles, and a ready smile just for her. Resisting the appeal of that smile was beyond her. She should do the hit it and quit it and ignore him. She should. But she wasn't going to.

She was going to be kicking herself as an idiot the whole flight home.

Still, once she was home, she had no reason to see him again. The divorce would be handled by their lawyers. She had no idea if they'd have to spend a day in court to finalize it, but that was hardly the place to spark up old romance. Nope, once she escaped Rome, she could forget about any pitter-pattering her heart and hormones might be doing. She'd have a new job and a new life to focus on. Of course, all that changed if she was pregnant, but she wasn't going to borrow trouble by thinking about that now.

She fluffed her short waves. "Since we have all day, I was thinking I would do some sightseeing."

"Let me guess." He stroked his fingers down his jaw as if thinking deeply. "We've already done the Capitoline, so I'm going to say the Vatican Museum and the *Palazzo Altemps.*"

What did it say about her that he could anticipate her so easily? "Eventually all of those, yes, but I was planning to start a little closer to home."

He snapped his fingers. "The Santa Maria basilica, right here in the *Trastevere.*"

"Give the man a cookie." She took off down the hall and he easily kept stride.

"Cookies, yum." He slapped a palm over his growling stomach. "Could I entice you into stopping at a bakery on the way? My treat."

"Sure." The elevator opened and an older couple stepped out. They nodded as they passed. Since the car was already there, Karen stepped in. The small space felt microscopic when Tate's big body occupied half of it. She twisted her lips. "You know, you don't have to spend the day with me if you don't want to. Maybe you want to see other things. Or just hang out with Gio."

His gaze darkened and his mouth tightened, but he said lightly, "Nope. I like those museums and churches. I'd like to revisit them too."

"Well, I won't try to stop you, then." She kept her gaze glued to the floor numbers as they crawled by at a snail's pace. "I didn't want you to feel obligated because of what we did last night."

"I don't feel obligated," Tate said, posture stiff and words stiffer. "I just want to check out the sights and I wouldn't mind the company."

After plucking a pair of sunglasses out of her purse, she slid them on. "Okay, then. Let's hit a bakery."

The elevator door opened. He waved his arm. "After you."

The heat of him enveloped her as he fell into step behind her, and she was intensely aware of his nearness. She'd had him several times the night before and still wanted another go. *Later,* she promised herself. She had the whole rest of her trip to indulge in that particular forbidden fruit. Juicy, tempting, and so sweet.

A bite of breakfast and they were off for the day.

It was magical. They wandered through all their favorite spots, the bridge they liked over the Tiber River, the old café where he'd taken her on their first date, the museum they'd gone to on their second date.

Some of the places were exactly the same, but some had changed. She was glad for that reality check. It had been more than a decade since they'd been here. It wasn't the exact same city, just as they weren't the exact same people.

Nothing would ever be the same again.

As bittersweet as the nostalgia was, she didn't want to be the college co-ed she'd been back then. That girl had stars in her eyes, blinded by the romance of it all. She wasn't a cynic now, but she had maturity and experience only time could grant. She liked herself as she was, liked who she was growing into. This year had been one of intense change. Since she'd broken up with Tate at Christmas, the New Year had ushered in a new life. She'd tried for years to content herself with the lonely marriage they'd had, but breaking out of that rut had been good for her. Painful, yes, but independence had its rewards. She had the career she'd always wanted, and moving to a smaller town had brought a position with more responsibility, but a slower pace of life.

Her existence would never be perfect, but it would always be changing. She just needed to steer that change in the direction she wanted.

It seemed fitting somehow to say a final goodbye to a relationship that had shaped her so deeply, in the city where it had all started.

chapter
seven

T ate took a swig of beer and watched Giovanni across the large pizza they shared. Gio had decided he needed to escape all the family and wedding chaos, so he'd shown up unannounced at Tate's door. Luckily, he'd stayed in Karen's room the night before and had just returned to his own room to shower and change. They'd invited her to join them, but she'd waved them off and gone to help Valentina deal with her family of drama-queens.

He hated to admit it to himself, but he wasn't sure if Karen was happy or disappointed to lose a day alone with him. The wedding was tomorrow, and he'd managed to invite himself along on all Karen's tourist excursions. He'd also ruthlessly steered her toward places they'd visited together, places where they'd gotten to know each other, where they'd fallen in love. If reminding her how good they'd once been together made her start thinking they might be good together again, then all the better.

He'd also asked for her input on a few things he wanted to do with his law firm. Not much and not often, because there was a delicate balance between wanting her to know her opinion mattered to his future plans, and making her continue to think he was like his father and couldn't shut off the obsessive workaholic side of himself long enough to enjoy a vacation. Tricky. Very tricky.

As if he'd read Tate's mind, Gio asked, "How's the campaign going?"

Pretending not to know what his friend was talking about, Tate raised an eyebrow. "The campaign?"

"To win back your wife, of course."

Tate sighed. "I have no idea."

"Come on, *amico mio*." Gio's glance was scolding. "I've seen the looks, the touching when you thought no one was looking. You're trying to get her back. Don't lie."

"I'm not lying and I'm not denying that I'm trying to reconcile with Karen." Tate waved his beer bottle in a dismissive arc. "I'm telling you I have no idea how well it's going."

"Ah. I misunderstood."

"Imagine that," he drawled.

Giovanni was silent for a few minutes, taking a bite of his pizza and chewing slowly. A frown puckered his brow. "How can you not know?"

"Americans aren't as good at reading women's minds as Italians, apparently."

He nodded sagely. "Yes, I've noticed it's one of your countrymen's many deficiencies."

Tate couldn't help a laugh. "Indeed."

The other man narrowed his eyes. "You have slept together again."

"I'm not giving you details, but yes. We have." Often and in very creative positions. There was a sense of discovery and playfulness to their love making that hadn't been there in years. God, it was amazing. Mind-blowing. And he needed to stop thinking about this or he was going to embarrass himself in public.

"Speaking of deficiencies..." Tate held his bottle of *Nastro Azzurro* aloft. "This is the best Italy has to offer for beer? Thank God for German imports, that's all I can say."

"It's good!" Gio took a deep swig of his beer.

Tate shot his friend a pitying look. "Yeah, keep telling yourself that."

Giovanni scoffed. "As if Americans do it better."

"We have some great microbreweries, but the big brands? Nasty. As I said, thank God for German imports." Tate smirked. "At least I can admit it though."

"Italians are wine specialists," Gio replied superciliously. "We leave the peasant drinks to our northern neighbors."

"Careful you don't say that in front of Karen." Tate stabbed his fork into an errant olive that had escaped his slice of pizza. "One of her best friends is dating a native German. Probably going to marry him too. Karen's very protective of her friends."

"Including my Valentina, yes. We've always been glad of your friendship. We wouldn't have each other without the two of you." Gio's expression went from sincere to cocky. "Of course, after this trip, you will have to say the same about Valentina and me."

"Isn't it bad luck to say such a thing?" Tate popped the olive into his mouth and chewed. "She hasn't agreed to take me back."

"Yet." Gio crossed himself and muttered something toward the heavens before refocusing on Tate. "It will be fine. You love each other. Trust in that."

"I'm trying."

The bottom line was, Karen had been adamant that this was just an affair. Whether she was softening that stance was less certain. Tate had never been the type to rely on fate or destiny, but this wasn't a trial and Karen wasn't a witness he could cross-examine into saying the wrong thing. This was far more important, and thus far more terrifying. He was walking a tightrope over an abyss, and at any moment, he could fall.

And yet, he was having the time of his life. For the first time in recent memory, he was enjoying himself. It was bliss. Being away from the family firm, being with Karen—it was right next door to nirvana.

Now if only he could hold on to this feeling forever.

"So." The Italian grinned. "Valentina and I decided not to have separate stag nights. Everyone who wants to come will join us at a *discoteca*. Fast music, dirty dancing—what could be more perfect before we wed?"

"If Valentina's grandmother gets down and dirty, I may never recover," Tate quipped.

Gio shuddered. "She is a wise woman and has opted out of this party."

"Thank God."

"*Sì*, I could not agree more," he added fervently. "She wishes to look her best at the wedding, so she wants her beauty rest. Valentina and I will take our older relatives out for dinner tonight, so they don't feel they miss out on special time with us. Then, dancing for the rest of our guests."

"I'll be there, of course." And with any luck, he'd be getting down and dirty with Karen on the dance floor. Nothing like some fully-clothed, full-body contact to rev you up for naked fun later. Which was something else he hadn't made time for since he passed the bar exam.

"Of course, your wife will be there too." Gio smiled. "I promise not to look—or comment—if you should break public decency laws while dancing together."

"Ha." Tate aimed his beer bottle at his friend. "You and Valentina are more likely to get arrested for that than we are. I've been to a club with you before, remember."

The other man rolled his shoulders in a shrug. "I know how to show a lady a good time."

There was no way in hell Tate was going to touch that comment, so he dug into his pizza and let the conversation peter out. Definitely for the best. Tate and Karen had spent their year in Rome as room-mates to Gio and Valentina, respectively, so they'd both listened to the passionate fights and loud make-up sex the couple had. As Karen had once mentioned—at that volume, there was no doubt that Valentina was enjoying herself.

Tate had no desire to reminisce on those old times.

There was no escaping him. Karen tried to hold in a groan. Tate had some sort of freakish sixth sense about when she was going to try to avoid him.

Or maybe she just wasn't trying that hard.

She cringed as that thought rang with painful truth. They shared a cab to the dance club Valentina and Giovanni had picked for their joint stag night. How Tate had known exactly when Karen would step out of her room to leave, she had no idea. But a tingle had gone through her body as he'd taken in her outfit.

She had not dressed to impress him. She had *not*.

Tugging down the hem of her microscopic midnight blue dress, she stared out the window. It was just a good dress to dance in, that was all. It had a racerback and a high neckline, so she was unlikely to experience a wardrobe malfunction while bouncing around. The ruching up the sides complemented her figure, the shortness of the skirt made her legs appear longer than they actually were, and there was nothing wrong with looking nice. That didn't mean it was for anyone other than herself—a confidence booster.

But the look in his eyes had made the extra effort on her appearance worth it. Wasn't that the stupidest thing ever? His opinion shouldn't matter in any way on anything. She wrinkled her nose at her reflection.

"We're almost there." He spoke for the first time since they'd gotten in the taxi.

She smoothed a hand over her dress. "Okay."

"You're quiet. Was everything all right with the family today?"

"Yes, of course." She felt his gaze on her, but didn't look at him. "The De Rossi clan has always been lovely to me. We still exchange Christmas cards, even twelve years after I left."

The backseat seemed to get smaller and more intimate, his voice low and warm. "I'm glad you got to see them."

"Me too. Especially while her grandmother was still around and had all her faculties in working order." A smile tugged at her lips. "That woman is fabulous."

"And terrifying."

A laugh trickled out of her. "All part of her charm."

He flicked his fingers against the tips of her hair. "Are you going to be terrifying as an old lady?"

She gave him an arch glance. "Naturally."

"Your grandma seemed pretty normal." His expression turned dubious. "I'm not sure you're genetically predisposed to be terrifying."

"Nature versus nurture." She shrugged, glad they were on a light topic. "Valentina's grandmother has nurtured my terrifying side."

"I guess time will tell on that one." His tone was so overly placating, she swatted his shoulder and he laughed. "So, how's your parents' road trip going? They're doing an RV trek across Canada, right?"

"Yep, to celebrate Dad's retirement." She bit her lower lip. "Their internet and cell phone connectivity is limited, which I think drove them nutty the first few weeks, but they seem to be enjoying the ability to unplug and reconnect with each other now. Mom says they're technologically roughing it for the first time since they were in the Peace Corps. I'm unsure if she meant that as a complaint or not."

He shook his head. "You know how my mother would mean it. Then again, she and my father would never have volunteered to camp in an RV. Or anywhere else that didn't have room service."

Their families had been so different on every possible level. The vast disparity in income levels had been the easiest hurdle to overcome when they'd married. Karen fiddled with the clasp on her slender evening bag. "Yeah, well. Ben says when this three-month jaunt is over, our parents will either be divorcing or renewing their vows."

"Renewing their vows, no doubt. Your parents are in it for the long haul."

"So are yours." Francesca and Robert were never splitting up, no matter how unhappy they were. But then again, maybe the life they had was their version of happiness. Karen didn't want to judge a relationship she wasn't in, but what they had was the antithesis of her idea of a good marriage. Unfortunately, it was almost the marriage she'd gotten. Relief swept through her at having escaped such a fate.

"Yeah, but your parents actually like each other." Tate reached out to brush a fingertip along her jawline, and she shivered with awareness. "I couldn't have asked for better in-laws."

Whereas she had tried to avoid hers as much as possible. "Thanks, I think."

"I wish I could have offered you better."

"I love Laurel," she replied sincerely. No need to bring up how little she'd liked his parents. They were just too different, too cold, too brittle. They weren't bad people, they just weren't her kind of people, and that had nothing to do with money or class.

"There you go." He tapped that finger against her chin. "I gave you the sister you never had. Though I think your best friends filled that gap long before Laurel did."

"There's always room for one more sister-friend." And Laurel had a fearlessness and outrageousness that had endeared her to Karen the moment they'd met.

"Good." There was a momentary pause. "Does your family know about you being here in Rome?"

"Yes, I emailed my brother and parents to let them know where I am. I mentioned you were here, and they were concerned your presence would upset me, but I assured them I was fine and said I was exploring my old foreign exchange haunts." She shifted on the seat. "I also spoke to my friends on Zoom."

"So they know everything."

It was a statement, not a question, but she answered anyway. "Yep. The drunken unprotected sex, the possible pregnancy, the unwise foreign affair. All of it."

He cleared his throat. "About the possible pregnancy. When will you—"

"In a few days, maybe." Not exactly a lie. Technically, she should have started her period today, but since she'd stopped taking the pill, she wasn't one hundred percent regular. "I'll tell you when I know anything."

That much was true, at least. She would never keep that kind of thing from anyone. Well, maybe if she'd had a boozy accidental one-night stand with an axe murderer. Then she probably wouldn't tell the father of her baby. And the kid would be told they had a goat herder for a dad. Or something like that.

"Thank you," he said.

She nodded. "Mmm-hmm."

"It's going to be okay. No matter what." He reached over, caught her hand, and squeezed her fingers. "Just remember that, all right?"

Her throat clogged with emotion she didn't want. The feeling of reassurance, of support from him, was so like it used to be that it sent a lance of sheer pain straight to her heart. *It's just an affair, Karen. Emotion has no place here. Knock it off.* She steeled herself and tugged her hand away. "You can stop with the touchy-feely supportiveness, Tate. It's not necessary."

"It's going to be necessary if you're pregnant," he stated flatly. "I'm not bailing out on any child of mine."

"I know. But that's not a discussion we need to have until we know something. Our chances are slim anyway, so let's not freak out unless we have to."

"So you're hoping you're not pregnant." The words were brittle, almost upset.

She stared at him. "You're hoping the same thing. You've never been particularly keen on having kids, and that's not even factoring in how this might complicate our divorce proceedings."

Instead of responding to her, he seemed to sigh in relief. "We're here."

"Fantastic." She was more than ready for this conversation to be over with. Because she wasn't sure at all if she didn't want to be pregnant with his child. She'd wanted that for so long—she'd wanted a lot of things for so long—and it was bittersweet to think it might happen after their marriage was over. Her logic told her she was a lot better off with an anonymous sperm donor, her heart said she wanted Tate as her baby-daddy.

It was tragic that bad she was off alcohol for the time being. She could use the biggest cocktail in history right about now.

Tate hopped out of the cab, held the door open and offered her a hand to help her stand on the uneven cobblestones. Her heels were higher and pointier than usual, but that was what one wore with a dress like this. She let him hold her arm until they got to the smooth flooring of the *discoteca* and then made herself slip away.

The wedding was tomorrow, she'd be gone a few days after that, and she just needed to calm down, get her rampaging emotions in check, and everything would be fine.

Striding into the club, she kept a look out for her friends. Of course, they were already out on the dance floor busting a move. She grinned as Valentina's hips swiveled in a way that flouted the laws of nature.

"*Amico mio!*" Gio shouted, giving Tate hug and an air-kiss on each cheek. He did the same to Karen.

Valentina grabbed her hands and twirled her in a little circle. They laughed, and Karen let the music take her away. The world narrowed down to hard bass, perspiration beading on her skin, and the visceral need to move.

The group formed a loose circle, Karen between two of Gio's female cousins. She didn't know how much time passed. After the first few songs, she was just dancing, giggling with everyone, shouting to be heard over the music as everyone made comments or joked or teased. Valentina's male cousin flirted with Karen outrageously, but that meant nothing to an Italian, and he was barely twenty years old. She was pretty sure men in this country started flirting from the cradle.

They broke into smaller pairs and trios as more people entered the club and hit the dance floor, making the place hot and sweaty, but energy was pulsing through the air. It was electric and fun and no one wanted to leave the floor. Tate and Gio went to get bottles of water for everyone else, but that was as close to a break as anyone took.

One song blended into another, and Karen glanced over to see the bride and groom tearing up the floor while hard music thumped through the massive room. The couple executed a few moves that Karen was pretty sure were illegal outside a strip joint. When she looked away, her gaze collided with Tate's.

Rolling his eyes, he looked amused. He took a step forward and bent to speak into her ear. "Only those two."

"Exactly. What were we thinking when we introduced them?"

He cracked up, as she'd known he would. He'd once asked her that same question in college when he'd had to dodge the Italian duo doing exhibitionist naughtiness in his living room. He gave her the answer she'd given him back then. "We thought they'd be perfect for each other. And we were right."

"No doubt." She nodded.

"Let's show them how it's done." He grabbed her hand and whipped her into a quick spin, then dipped her over his arm. She came up laughing, clinging to his neck. She'd forgotten that his parents had made him take ballroom dancing classes as a teen, and that he was pretty light on his feet. When he drew her arm over her head and whirled her around a few times, she went with it. This trip was supposed to be easy and fun, and that was all she'd let it be.

Tate guided her into a few more turns, his teeth flashing in a grin. When she bumped into Gio, he made a face at her. "You two are showing us up!"

"Poor baby." She stuck her tongue out at him.

Eyes shining with mirth, Valentina caught her fiancé's arm. "Come on. Less talking, more dancing!"

The two demonstrated a few wild antics, including one move that should have been reserved for a pole dancing routine, but then Valentina planted her mouth on Gio's and that pretty much meant he didn't care who was showing him up.

Tate leaned down and chuckled in Karen's ear. "At least neither of us has to share an apartment with them anymore, or we'd be in for some voyeurism tonight. Or would it be just exhibitionism? I think it would depend on how much you enjoy watching or being watched while you come, right?"

His breath rush over her skin as he spoke, cooling the perspiration there, and a shudder ran through her. Having him talk about coming while he was pressed against her back and she could feel every inch of his muscular body was sheer torture. They were still moving, still dancing, still in sync, but now the slow rub of him against her felt less playful and more provocative.

"What do you think, Karen?" His arm came around her and he splayed his fingers over her midriff.

Heat bubbled in her veins, and she let her head fall back on his shoulder. She felt his erection rise, pressing into her backside. What had he asked? How could he expect her to think about anything right now? "Um... No one's ever watched me come unless they were in bed with me."

"Ah." She heard a smile in his voice, and his tone deepened to pure sin. "Should I do less talking and more dancing too?"

"Yes." Dancing would be good—sweet friction, lovely fire burning within her, some muscles loosening, others tightening. The music filled her, made her move with him, against him, with no thought for anything or anyone else. There was no future, no past, just this moment with this man. Everything was hot sensation and shocking need. God, it felt good.

His fingertips began drifting along the midline of her stomach—down, down, down until he skimmed the edge of her lace panties, then up, up, up until he slid into her cleavage and she wished that he'd cup and squeeze her breasts, toy with her taut nipples. The rhythm of the song seeped into her blood, and her heart was racing. They rocked together, his hard shaft nudging into the cleft of her buttocks. Her sex clenched on emptiness, and shivers ran through her. She wanted, needed, craved.

"Tate," she whimpered. She caught his wandering hand, her nails digging into his flesh in an attempt to convey the lust rocketing through her body. "I want you. Please."

"Yes. Come with me." He latched onto her wrist and pulled her away from the dance floor. Not that she struggled, because she'd come with him anywhere at this point.

The bathroom was unisex, so either of them could use it, but she was guessing it wasn't supposed to have multiple people in it at the same time. He pushed her inside and locked the door behind them.

Her lungs heaved as she struggled to breathe. She should put a stop to this right now, but she wasn't going to. Sanity was far beyond her grasp. "If you don't have a condom with you, Patton, I will murder you for bringing me in here."

"Luckily, I'm covered." He fished a rubber out of his wallet and twirled it between his fingers. "Or I will be."

"Thank. *God*," she said.

His arm snaked around her waist and hauled her against him. He slammed his mouth down over hers, his tongue shoving between her lips. She fisted her fingers in his hair, matching him stroke for stroke as their tongues twined. Her excitement ratcheted higher and wetness slicked her sex. His thigh insinuated itself between hers, forcing her dress upward. The heavy muscles in his leg flexed, riding her sex into his thigh. Her hips snapped in a frantic rhythm, tingles skipping down her skin, the first shimmer of climax arcing through her. She threw her head back, sobbing for air, and he took the opportunity to bite and lick and suck his way down her throat.

"Tate, I need to... I'm going to..." The words trailed off in a shameless moan.

A growl rumbled from his chest as he ripped himself away from her. "Turn around and put your hands on the wall."

She was so far gone that she didn't even blink. Yes, she was absolutely going to get busy in a club bathroom. The tile was cold against her palms, sending a shiver through her that made her nipples peak tighter. She heard the rasp of his zipper as he unfastened his pants, the rip of him opening the condom, the rustle of him putting it on. With every second that passed, her need twisted inside her, her pulse pounding. He pushed her dress up until it bunched around her waist, then tugged her panties down just enough that they shackled her thighs together.

"I'm going to take you hard, Karen." His voice was harsh with lust, and that excited her too.

"Yes." Swift and maybe even a little rough was exactly what she craved.

It was the reverse of the night she'd tied him up, where she'd taken control. Tonight, she had no control—didn't need it, didn't want it. Now she was flying high on sensation, and she reveled in the pure feeling.

The head of his shaft probed at her entrance, and then he pierced her in one quick plunge. A cry burst from her as he stretched her, filled her. His arms came around her, his left hand teasing and pulling at her nipples, his right hand diving into her slick folds to torment her swollen nub. He pistoned in and out of her, his pelvis slapping against her backside.

It was hard and fast and took her to the edge of sanity in seconds. She tried to widen her stance, tilt her hips to take him deeper, but the way her underwear twisted around her legs kept her exactly where he'd put her. Maddening and perfect all at once. His fingers sweeping over her nub in time with his thrusts made her bite her lip to keep from screaming. The throb of music probably would have covered the noise for anyone who didn't have an ear pressed to the door, but she was beyond rationality. It was all reflex and reaction, sex and sweat.

"You have no idea how good it feels to be inside you," he growled.

A breathless laugh poured from her. "About as good as it feels to have you inside me, maybe?"

"Maybe, but somehow I doubt it." There was a smile in his voice when he spoke. "Let's see if we can make it feel even better."

He pinched her nub, and that was enough to spin her into ecstasy. Pinpricks of light exploded behind her eyelids, she came so hard. Her channel fisted around his plunging shaft, and each time he entered her sent another wave of orgasm crashing over her. She bowed her torso, pushing her hips back to meet his thrusts, more than willing to let this rush of sensation last as long as possible. His groans kissed her ears, the hitch to his breath telling her he was close to the edge, so she deliberately clenched her inner muscles around him.

"Karen!" A long, tortured moan ripped from his throat. He slammed deep, grinding his hips into her as he climaxed. Shudders racked him, shaking through her as well. They stayed that way for a long time, gasping for breath, shivers of completion passing through them. Karen dropped her forehead to one of the hands resting against the wall, her eyes sliding shut.

Tate kissed the back of her shoulder. "You are so amazing."

The gentle touch and the rough reverence in his voice made her heart skip a beat. *No.* None of that mushy stuff. Hot, sweaty shagging.

That was all. She pushed herself upright. "We need to get back."

"Yes." He sighed, and they both tidied themselves as best they could.

She shook her head. "We're officially crazy, you know."

"Yep." He heaved another sigh, the sound utterly satisfied.

"And way too old to be doing stuff like this." Someone had to point it out, so it might as well be her.

"No arguments here," he agreed cheerfully while zipping his pants. He cast her a sexy grin, his gaze dark and hooded. Bedroom eyes.

Awareness shimmered between them, even though she should be exhausted and fully satiated. "Want to go back to the hotel and do it again?"

His smile widened, his voice dropping to a sinful rumble. "I thought you'd never ask."

Her thighs quivered at that dark tone—the one he used when they were in bed together, urging her to further depths of depravity. She cleared her throat. "I think I have a headache from the loud music."

"I'll make our excuses." He held the door open for her. Thankfully, the short hallway was clear.

"Then I'll get in line for a cab."

Four more nights left. She intended to indulge herself before she got back to the reality of her new, single life. Her gaze dropped to Tate's sculpted ass as he preceded her down the hall. *Mm-hm.* The sex was as amazing as it had ever been, and she was determined to crush any other tender feelings that might be cropping up. Sex and chemistry, that was all.

And it was damn good.

CHAPTER EIGHT

The wedding day was a bittersweet kind of hell for Tate. Sure, he was thrilled for his friends and he got to sit next to Karen, which somehow made the whole thing a torturous reminder of everything that was both wrong and right with his life.

He still hadn't gotten up the balls to ask Karen to reconcile. The bottom line was, he was terrified to even try. There were moments where she seemed to soften toward him, and others where she clearly wanted distance. Emotional, if not physical. It was a white-hot blade to the heart to be used for sex by the woman he loved more than life itself. How the hell had he ended up his wife's sex toy? It would be laughable if it didn't hurt so much. Even if he deserved the pain, it didn't mean he enjoyed it. Masochism had never been his thing, and yet here he was, agonized and unable to make it stop. Looking forward to even a single moment in Karen's company, even if it pained him.

He really was a sick bastard.

Music swelled and he rose a half-beat behind everyone else as they watched the bride enter the cathedral. Karen leaned over and whispered in his ear while Valentina started down the aisle. "She was right. That is absolutely the perfect dress for her."

Yes, because it was over the top in a way that only she could pull off. She looked beautiful and stylish—she always did—but her gown was so avant garde, it was difficult to see it as a wedding dress. Well, it was white. Most of it anyway. It screamed drama, which meant it screamed Valentina. Perfect, indeed.

"It suits her." He nodded. The scent of Karen's perfume teased his nose—citrus and roses and something spicy. So familiar and so her. He glanced away, his attention catching on Giovanni's expression. "I have never seen Gio so nervous or so happy. That's how I felt on our wedding day."

What compelled him to insert that last part, he didn't know. She stiffened a bit beside him, and that made him ache. The conversation the night before about her potential pregnancy, and hearing her say she hoped they wouldn't have a child, had twisted something painful inside him.

Logically, he knew an unexpected pregnancy when he had so much ground to make up with her would only confuse things, but it had still hurt to have her say it. Maybe because she had always been vocal about wanting children, maybe because he'd only just figured out how much he wanted them too, maybe because it felt like he was losing ground with her, that hoping they might get back together was utterly futile. Then again, he still didn't know when or if he should tell her what he wanted. Should he make it clear he was angling for reconciliation? At what point would that idea not send her running? Was hiding his real motivation a lie of omission or good strategy for getting her in a receptive frame of mind? Christ, he had no clue. Every day that passed made everything more muddled, but left him more determined—okay, desperate—to win her over to his way of thinking.

"I hope their wedding and marriage has a happier ending than ours." She hastened to add, "But they're older and wiser than we were, which I'm sure makes all the difference in the world."

"True." He slanted a look at her. "I think I'd be more certain at my age that I found the right person than I was then, and I was pretty damn sure then."

She cast him a glance, as if unsure how to take his words. She didn't ask him to explain and he didn't offer. He'd known at twenty-one that he'd found the right woman when he'd met her, and he was just as sure now. No matter how badly he'd messed up, that was one thing he'd never doubted.

After Valentina reached Giovanni's side, the guests resumed their seats. The lengthy Catholic ceremony gave Tate time to think, to consider, to make some decisions. He needed to be upfront with Karen, ask her to take him back, beg her for a second chance. Hopefully, this week had warmed her to the idea, but he was never going to know unless he manned up and laid his cards on the table.

The question was—when? He had three days until they flew back to the States. Should he have The Talk today, after the wedding, or let himself use the time he had left to continue to make his case?

He tensed when Karen set her hand on his leg. Her fingers stroked gentle circles—up, down. From the outside of his knee to the inside of his thigh. Almost reaching his shaft, but not quite. It was a subtle teasing that had him sweating, fire beginning to pump through his veins. His shaft stiffened to an uncomfortable semi-erection, and there wasn't a single thing he could do about it except endure the torment. As non-family, they were sitting toward the back, so he doubted anyone would notice them, but still.

Leaning down let him whisper in her ear. "You realize this is a church, right?"

"Mmm-hmm." Her nail ran along his inseam.

He swallowed hard, trying to urge his body not to respond. As if there was a hope in hell of that happening. "Lightning is going to strike."

A half-smile tilted one corner of her full lips. "I note you're not doing anything to stop me, Patton."

No, he wasn't, was he? A soft snort escaped him. "You are gonna get it later."

"Looking forward to it," she murmured.

Ah, Christ. He closed his eyes, shaking his head. Carnal images flooded his mind, making the semi-erection turn into the real thing. He was going to embarrass himself when he stood up if he didn't stop her. The slow caresses would drive him mad. He caught her wandering hand. "Okay, that's all I can handle."

"Aw, how sad." She bumped her shoulder against his. "This ceremony is long, boring, and my Italian isn't good enough to catch everything."

"Agreed." He brought her palm to his mouth, kissed the center, then bit the base of her thumb. Her breath caught, and he grinned. He loved how quickly and easily she reacted for him. Then again, he did the same for her, didn't he?

"Oh, good." A soft sigh made her chest swell against the bodice of her dress. "We're getting to the kissing part. That means it's almost over, right?"

"God, I hope so."

She smothered a laugh. "We're terrible."

"Hey, our ceremony was over in ten minutes. Fifteen, tops." He shrugged unapologetically. "We've been sitting here for an hour, at least."

"Eighty-three minutes." She tilted her wrist to show him the delicate bracelet-watch. "I clocked it."

"Jeez." No wonder his butt was starting to go numb on the wooden pew.

"Soooo ready for the reception."

"And the food." As if on cue, his stomach growled. He'd rolled her under him first thing this morning, and they'd had to scramble to get ready and make it to the wedding. No breakfast for them, but it had been completely worth it.

He kept her hand in his when the wedding finished and they filed out behind the bridal couple. Karen didn't try to pull away, but Tate wasn't sure if that meant anything other than she didn't want to draw attention now that they weren't sitting safely behind everyone else.

Yeah, it was time to have it out. This will-she-won't-she debate in his head wouldn't achieve anything more than driving him insane. He needed to know where they stood, if he had even the slimmest hope of winning her back.

And he'd thought asking her to marry him was the most terrifying question he'd ever asked.

"Darling!" Valentina held her arms open and Karen stepped into them, returning the embrace.

She bent awkwardly at the waist to reach her friend. "I'm afraid to crush your dress."

"Isn't it perfect?" Valentina stroked her hand down the exquisite bodice. She glowed with joy, taking her from beautiful to utterly breathtaking.

Karen nodded. "I told you it was during your fitting, but somehow it's even better today."

"Yes, it is." Tears brightened Valentina's eyes, a smile curving her red-tinted lips. "My grandmother said I was even more gorgeous than she was on her wedding day."

From a rather vain old lady, that was saying a lot. Karen waggled her eyebrows. "The highest possible compliment."

"Truly, yes." Valentina winked.

They chuckled, and she tapped her champagne flute against Karen's glass. Karen held a tumbler of orange juice, which she figured everyone assumed was a screwdriver cocktail. That was fine with her. She didn't want questions she couldn't answer. "The reception is fabulous."

Giovanni's parents were hosting the event, and their home was absolutely gorgeous. Not huge, but it was clear where the man got his sense of style. They'd had lunch catered by Valentina's favorite Moroccan restaurant, and now guests were mingling while waiters circulated with trays loaded down with teeny desserts from Gio's favorite *pasticceria*.

The bride flashed her dimples. "Did you try the miniature tiramisu?"

"I think I've tried one of everything." Karen slapped a hand over her stomach. "I've eaten too much, but it's so good I can't stop."

"That's exactly how we want our guests to feel about the food." Satisfaction oozed from the other woman.

A loud guffaw drew their attention, and Karen saw the priest holding his middle in a belly laugh while he spoke to Tate. God, Tate was good-looking—all dark hair and golden skin. He'd been outside enough this week that he'd tanned deeply, and his teeth shone white in contrast when he smiled.

Valentine leaned close. "The priest is Gio's uncle, you know."

"I heard." The man was a shorter, pudgier, balder version of the groom.

"He hates it when I make altar boy jokes."

Karen cast her an incredulous glance. "You don't."

"I do." Valentina snickered.

"Shame on you. That's so bad."

She hummed in agreement. "Maybe Gio will spank me for it."

"I thought you wanted to do the spanking." Karen nudged her friend. "You were testing the swing of that pink riding crop like you intended to use it yourself."

The bride sipped her champagne. "I am—how do you Americans say it?—equal opportunity."

Karen snorted and decided it was safer not to comment.

After a brief pause, Valentina said, "Tate's looking better than I've seen him in a long time. He was always hot, but...Italy is good for him, I think."

"Taking the first vacation in a decade will relax a man," Karen replied with as mild a tone as she could manage. Getting laid on a regular basis might also contribute to his mellow frame of mind.

"Gio tells me he's quit his father's law firm and will start his own. This is a good thing."

"Yeah." Karen went from mild to noncommittal. "Good for him."

Valentina tilted her head. "You're also looking very good, less sad than you did the day you arrived."

Karen couldn't prevent a flinch, as if her friend had prodded her with a hot poker. "Oh."

"I think Italy is good for you too. Or maybe it's just Tate who's good for you."

"Valentina. Stop." She sighed. "This is your wedding day. It's all about you. Take shameless advantage of that. Forget about my marital problems. Or my lack of marital problems, since I have no marriage."

The bride's lips firmed in a stubborn line. "You are good together. I want you to be as happy as I am. You could have that with him, now that he's turned his life around."

Now that *was* giving an old wound a hot poker prod. Karen's tone went sharper than she intended. "Is it turned around? Tell me starting his own firm won't make him just as bad as he was before. Always at the office, total workaholic."

Valentina's mouth opened, closed. "I think he will not let that happen."

"I think he didn't mean to let it happen with his father's firm. Or so he said the day he proposed. Life doesn't always go according to plan." Truer words had never been spoken.

"No, sometimes it goes better. If you let it." She wagged a finger in Karen's face. "There's still love there. I see it in your eyes. Love is something you should not throw away."

"Are we done arguing?" Karen arched her eyebrows, refusing to be drawn into this discussion further. No one would win, and it would just upset her and make her dwell on all the failings of her marriage and whether it was worth it to try again. It wasn't. She knew that, no matter what her stupid heart or unruly hormones might say. She offered the bride a gamine grin. "And did I mention you look pretty today?"

Frustration crossed her friend's face. She continued shaking that admonishing finger. "Stubborn."

"Look who's talking," Karen shot back, crossing her arms.

Valentina burst into laughter. "True. But remember what I said. Now come with me."

Because she turned away from Tate and all the turmoil and temptation he engendered just by standing there, Karen didn't hesitate to scurry after the other woman. By the time she caught up, Valentina was rooting around a mess of bags and boxes in her in-laws' guest bedroom.

"Here, this is for you." She held out a gift, then pulled back. "Don't unwrap it now. My family likes to look into any open box. The priest too."

The box was light, but the wickedness on her face made Karen shake her head. "It's something dirty, isn't it?"

The bride crinkled her nose prettily. "But, of course, darling! It is me, yes?"

"Yes." If anyone had a claim to eternal naughtiness, it was Valentina.

She winked, tapping a finger against the top of the present. "To help you enjoy *la Bella Italia*. And perhaps Tate too."

Karen's eyes narrowed, but Valentina's expression was guileless. Always a bad sign. But without opening the gift, there was no way to know what might be inside. Sex toys? Slutty lingerie? A riding crop of her own?

"Pick this up before you go." Valentina took the present back and set it on a shelf. Then she headed outside to the garden, where her guests were gathered. A waiter took their empty glasses, and she glanced over her shoulder as she walked. "Gio booked two nights for us at Grand Hotel de la Minerve. It was less expensive to do it that way and leave for the honeymoon a day later. He's a romantic, but not a fool with his money. Which I like because you know I'm an expensive woman." Her eyes twinkled. "I can't complain, in any case—I've always wanted to stay at that hotel. We have a couple's massage tomorrow, and then room service all day. You and I must say goodbye today, darling, because I don't intend to let him out of bed until we have to run to the airport."

Karen hooked her arm through her friend's. "Good plan."

"Isn't it?" A single eyebrow rose, and Valentina bit her lower lip, the picture of wickedness. "Giovanni will need to work to keep up with me. But he's up to the task, I think."

Unable to prevent a laugh, Karen hugged the other woman. "It's been so good to see you again."

"Yes." Valentina squeezed her tight, then held her at arm's length. "I've told you how happy I am that you could come, haven't I? It meant so much to me to have you here."

"I'm glad I made it over." More than glad. She'd been long overdue for a visit. She loved Italy, always had, always would. "I'll even have a few days to get over the jetlag before I start my new job."

"It's always easier to adjust flying west than east," Valentina said bracingly.

Karen tilted her head and responded drolly, "That's good, or they're going to wonder why they hired me as library director."

"But you're the boss now. I'm excited for you!"

"Thanks." She couldn't keep the pride from her voice. She was good at what she did, and this promotion justified her years of hard work. One of the things that had drawn Tate and her together was their ambition, but Karen could turn it off. Tate had never been able to. "I think I'm going to like the new position, even if Half Moon Bay's library system is smaller than Palo Alto's. HMB is home, and I'm glad to be back. My parents and best friends are there. I think my brother wants to settle there after college too."

"Does Ben know what he wants to do?"

Karen groaned. "Lawyer."

"No!" The other woman's eyes widened.

"Yes."

A laugh tinkled from Valentina. "You're surrounded."

"Not with Tate and his family out of the picture." Karen jutted her chin pugnaciously. "Now, there's just Ben. Assuming he really does finish law school."

The bride stuck out her tongue. "Tate is clearly not out of the picture. He's standing right over there."

"When I board that plane for California, he is. After that, he can talk to my divorce attorney."

"If he doesn't talk you out of it," Valentina retorted. "Gio and I have had our problems over the years—nothing as bad as what you dealt with, of course—but there were times I considered leaving him. But I never did because I thought: do I truly believe I'll find a man who fits me better than him? The answer has always been no. So...do you truly think you'll find a man who suits you better than Tate?"

"I'm not a fortune teller, Valentina. There's no way I can know that."

She pinned Karen with a stare. "Remember there is risk no matter what you choose. You only see the risk of being hurt if you take him back and it's bad. But there's also the risk that you throw him away and never find anyone as good. You already have a man who loves you, and who you love in return. That's the most important part. Isn't that precious enough to hold on to?"

Karen's lips formed a moue. "I thought Gio made a deal about not pressuring either of us."

Valentina's fingers moved in graceful arcs. "Yes, but as you said, it's my day and I should take shameless advantage of it."

How could Karen not laugh at that? Her own words turned against her. "Touché."

CHαpTer NINe

K aren was late.

Yeah, she was running late meeting Tate, but worse: she was officially *late*. As in, she should definitely have started her period by now and hadn't. As in, she might be pregnant. She hurried along the cobblestone walkway and her stomach executed a nauseating roll that she absolutely refused to believe might be morning sickness. She told herself not to panic, not to assume anything. Her cycle wasn't being regulated by birth control anymore, so that meant fluctuations could happen. But still, she should have started two or three days ago. Nothing so far. No spotting, no bloating, no signs of the impending monthly.

Another rollercoaster-style belly twist, but it was followed by a flutter of excitement. And...maybe...hope? Yes, she wanted kids. Always had. So, even though it would be inconvenient and no doubt difficult to entwine her life with Tate's in a fundamental, genetic way that a divorce could do nothing to sever, she would welcome a child that came from this affair. She would love the baby with her whole heart, and she'd just have to put on her big girl panties when it came to dealing with any problems or discomfort that cropped up from her continued contact with Tate.

She refused to consider that some of her excitement sparked from having that possible connection to Tate. Nope, the enthusiasm was just for the baby she'd always wished for. Period.

And there was Tate, waiting for her in front of the movie theater. She knew the moment he saw her, because his face lit, smiling in a way that he reserved just for her. It told her she was special, loved. No. She forced that treacherous thought away. It was just sex. If she was so special or loved, she would have been a priority for him and they wouldn't be divorcing. She needed to remember that. It didn't matter what her hormones said, her logic would win that argument every time. No sex was good enough to put up with the life she used to lead.

Not that he'd said anything about wanting her back—Julie and Valentina had said that, not Karen's soon-to-be-ex. Karen and Tate were boarding separate planes tomorrow, and there'd been no mention of wanting more than short-term sex, so she needed to slow her freak out. She had enough to worry about without borrowing trouble.

Then again, she hadn't exactly encouraged any deep discussions, had she? Nope, she'd actively avoided them. So even if Tate had wanted to have some kind of heart-to-heart, she'd made sure he got no opportunities.

"Hey, you." He popped a quick kiss on her cheek, then turned to hold the theater door open for her. "I bought tickets to the movie you wanted already. Let's go."

She'd picked the romantic comedy instead of the action flick they were showing, which Tate had accepted stoically. He might be a pretty cultured guy, but he loathed a chick flick as much as the next red-blooded American man. Too bad—if he wanted to sit next to her for a movie, he'd have to suck it up.

Mean, yeah, but hey...it was her vacation, so she could do what she wanted. No one was twisting his arm to make him join her. That was his choice. And maybe she wanted him to prove he'd put up with whatever she had to dish out, since he'd put her through so much during their marriage. She sighed, not liking what that realization said about her. Maybe he deserved it, but she should be beyond such pettiness.

Ah, well. She was human.

The movie theater looked the same as it had twelve years ago. A little more run down, but essentially unchanged. Nice. Once upon a time, they'd loved this place because it played movies in English and they'd both been homesick for America and didn't want to admit it.

They slipped into the already darkened theater and found seats just as the opening credits were rolling. Hey, they'd missed the boring previews, so her lateness was actually great timing. Go her.

Now all she had to do was find a home pregnancy test and break the final news to Tate, one way or the other. The movie wasn't good enough to hold her attention—it was cringe-worthy, in fact—so her thoughts circled around the maybe-baby and how or when she should admit she was supposed to have started her period.

Okay, enough already. She tried to regroup and focus on the film, which might have been a mistake, because really watching it made it worse. Or made it clear just how bad it was. Wow, this comedy blew.

"No wonder this one tanked in the box office." Tate's breath ruffled the tiny hairs at the base of her neck, and she shivered.

Silently, she agreed with him. This was quite possibly the saddest movie of all time. It tried to be funny but wasn't. The guy was an unlikable dude-bro who was clearly a pointless waste of space, and the woman tried to be witty but the dialogue delivery was so bad she just sounded like a catty bitch. They might be perfect for each other, but Karen couldn't care less if they ended up together at this point. They could Thelma and Louise off a cliff for all she cared. Actually, that might make the movie more interesting. Saddest. Movie. Ever.

Tate grunted. "If he gives that goofy-ass laugh one more time—"

Whatever threat he was going to make was cut off by the actor's goofy-ass laugh. Tate's head fell back against his seat and Karen was pretty sure he whimpered like a mortally wounded animal.

Since the film was her pick, she felt the need to defend it, no matter how much she agreed. "Maybe the ending is good."

"It could only be good if they died in a fiery explosion."

The comment eerily echoed her previous thought. She didn't like that they were so in tune. They'd been out of sync in every possible way for a long time. His hand curled around hers and it felt too good, too natural. Her chest squeezed and her stomach roiled. Emotions again. Feelings she'd been shoving away for days. If she were brutally honest, she'd admit that what scared her most was that her traitorous, stupid heart felt the same as it had when they'd first come to Italy, as if she were falling in love all over again.

As if the last eight years of suffering hadn't happened.

It was insane. It was terrifying.

It made her want to curl up and cry.

"I need to get out of here." She grabbed her purse and shot from her seat.

Tate didn't say a word, just stayed hot on her heels as she bolted for the door. She pushed out into the cool evening air and sucked in slow, even breaths. *Calm down, Karen. Just calm down. You're okay. Everything is going to be fine.*

If she told herself that often enough, maybe it would be true.

T ate forced himself not to demand what was wrong.

   She wanted to walk back to the hotel and she didn't want to talk, so he kept pace with her and kept his mouth shut. It was damn hard. Something clearly wasn't right, and he'd be a fool if he thought it wasn't about them, but he sensed pushing right now would end in disaster. Doing nothing went against the grain, but he did it anyway.

Even more frustrating, he'd tried to bring up the topic of reconciliation twice since wedding, but she was an expert at distraction—funny quips that made them laugh and changed the subject, hot seduction that left him mindless with lust, rushing off to see another tourist attraction, which put them in too public a setting for that kind of conversation. It was as if she knew what he wanted and didn't want him to ask. Maybe that thought was pure paranoia or just plain fear, but he couldn't help thinking that way.

Karen's brow furrowed and her gaze was on her feet, as if each step on the uneven cobblestone streets of the *Trastevere* required her full attention. Whether she realized it or not, she was trusting him to watch out for her. If she were alone, she'd be more alert to the normal dangers inherent to city living—speeding cars, muggers, or worse. The small display of trust, even if unconsciously done, was a good sign. He wanted her trust back, badly.

When she made a wrong turn, he set his hand on her waist and guided her back in the hotel's direction. "We'll be there soon, sweetheart."

Nodding, she gave him a quick glance, and he read the turmoil there.

What could he say? How could he make this better? A familiar helplessness closed around him, choking him. It had been a decade of not knowing what to do or say to fix things between them. Failure coated his tongue.

He blew out a breath. "Let's get you back. Maybe take a hot bath, and I'll run to the gelato place next to the hotel and get some of that chocolate chip flavor you like—*stracciatella*."

"That sounds nice, actually." Her mouth worked for a moment. "Sorry I freaked out back there."

He shrugged, spotting their hotel as they turned the last corner. "It was a bad movie anyway. I was glad to leave."

"Yeah."

An awkward silence fell between them, and he scrambled to find something to fill it. "Valentina and Gio's flight should have taken off by now."

"If he could pry her out of bed." A little grin formed on her lips. "She's always wanted to stay at the Grand Hotel de la Minerve."

The smile made some of the tightness in his chest ease. He kept his tone light. "Yep, and even with the slight delay before they left town, the hotel means no crazy family, just them. He's a smart man."

She nodded. "Though it is a long flight to Bora Bora, she'll be happy to try out her new bikinis."

Tate cocked a brow, angling her a sardonic look. "Should I ask how much fabric is involved in these bathing suits? Or, rather, how little?"

"Probably not." Karen tapped a fingertip against her lips. "She's not quite ready for a day at the nudist beach, but she's close."

"He's not only a smart man, but a lucky one," he replied, sotto voce.

"A sentiment he'd agree with wholeheartedly."

He snorted. "With a few added details about his brilliance. Shy and retiring, Gio is not."

"Nor Valentina." She tipped her palms up in a philosophical shrug.

"We really did good with those two." He patted her shoulder. "Nutty as they are, they do fit."

"Yeah, they fit like a blowtorch and gasoline. Explosive." The first full smile of the evening unfurled on her mouth.

He laughed. "Right."

Pausing at the window of the shop next to the hotel, she peered inside. "I think I'd like my gelato now. The *stracciatella* is calling my name."

"Hmm." He held the door open for her, and the alluring scent of her perfume filled his nose as she swept past. "I can understand the appeal, but I need a final dose of the amarena cherry gelato. No one back home does it quite like they do."

She stepped to the end of the short line at the counter. "Sadly, the best place I've found for pistachio gelato in our area is Costco. Though I admit I haven't looked very hard."

"My mother would be horrified you shop there." He rolled his eyes at himself. As if he needed to bring up his family right now.

They reached the counter and placed their orders. A few minutes later, they had bowls of cold, creamy goodness and a spot at a small table by the window.

He'd hoped she'd let the mother comment slide, but after they'd sat, she quipped, "Maybe I should bring Francesca a quart of the stuff and tell her it's from some chichi new place. Bet she'd love it."

"Ha." He took a bite of the tart cherry confection. "I'd love to see the expression on her face when you told her."

"Like she sucked a lemon, no doubt." She wrinkled her nose, then shrugged. "But, you know, for all her snobbery, she never seemed to care that I didn't grow up in the country club crowd. She's not a warm and fuzzy person, but she's not unkind either."

At least she had something good to say about his utter mess of a family. He was glad she had a few pleasant memories, since he hoped they'd stay her in-laws. "Mother's got her nicer points. Well-off doesn't necessarily mean asshole."

She smirked. "No, Francesca left the assholery to your father."

"Indeed." Yeah, he'd seen that one coming. Karen and his dad had gotten along well enough, but she was entirely justified in resenting his father's role in the breakdown of their marriage. The worst part was, Dad could see what was going on and he just didn't care. Blind ambition and bullheadedness were stock in trade for Robert Patton. "Is 'assholery' a real word?"

"It is now." She stabbed her spoon at him to punctuate the point.

The shop had cleared out until there was only one other couple, who were busy making eyes at each other on the far side of the *gelateria*. Since it was quiet and relatively private, he ventured to ask, "Do you want to talk about it?"

"Hmm." She licked a bit of gelato from her thumb. "You know...I'd really rather show you the present Valentina gave me."

Curiosity piqued inside him, because any gift from Valentina that put a naughty glint in Karen's gaze had to be good, but he quashed it. "We could do both. Show and tell."

Her expression sobered. "No. I really, truly do not want to talk about anything intense, Tate. If that means you want to bail on the last night with me, I understand."

The quaver in her voice made him hesitate. Familiar frustration flooded him—not knowing what to do. The irony was sharp. He was the epitome of confidence in the courtroom, but with his wife he was an insecure, tongue-tied mess. At least when it came to serious topics.

"Do you want me to bail?" He locked his gaze with hers, all but daring her to look away.

Her throat worked as she swallowed hard. "No, but I also don't want A Talk."

"This isn't the last night, though, Karen," he pointed out. "We have several intense conversations that still need to happen."

"Right, the divorce settlement stuff." She nodded.

"And the baby."

Her face paled, every inch of color draining away.

"Do you have anything you want to tell me about that?" His gut clenched as he realized what might be bothering her. Perhaps it wasn't their relationship, per se, but the consequences of what they'd done.

She shook her head so hard, the short strands of her hair flew out in a cloud around her face. Her gaze dropped to the tabletop. "No, nothing is certain yet. Still."

A lie. After twelve years of knowing her, he could spot falsehoods when she told them. She was rarely dishonest, and maybe this was more denial than true dishonesty. Denial about the possibility of a child. Meaning she thought she might be pregnant. Something hot and sweet burned his chest, flooding him with...hope. God, yes, he wanted to see her lovely body ripen with his baby, wanted to cradle that child in his arms, hold its finger when it learned to walk, hold his breath and pray when that kid learned to drive.

He sucked in a lungful of air, contained the burgeoning swell of excitement. "Okay, so...that's something we have to discuss when we get home, right?"

"Right." She lifted a spoonful of gelato to her mouth, and he noted her fingers trembled.

"I have to admit, I'm glad this isn't the last night we'll see each other." Time to push, just a bit. "It's been nice to reconnect and remember the good times we've had together. Our marriage wasn't all bad."

"No, it wasn't." Her gaze softened, but then her lips firmed into a stubborn line. "But at the end, it wasn't very good either."

"True." He sat back in his chair. "I wish I could change that."

"You can't." Her eyes narrowed, letting him know he was treading on shaky ground.

To press his case or not? The clock was ticking down before they left Rome, but as he'd pointed out, they'd still have to deal with each other stateside.

"The past is definitely something I can't change, you're right." He took a final bite of the amarena and set his dish aside. "However, I can work on shaping the future into something better, can't I?"

"It's your future, so sure, make it better." Her spoon clinked against her bowl as she finished too. Her lips twisted and she sighed. "I hope you're happy, Tate. Really. Good luck with everything."

The finality in her voice made his gut clench and, sue him, but he took the easy way out. "Me too. I hope we're both happy. Now, about that present from Valentina..."

CHAPTER TEN

The sway of her hips lured him like a Lorelei as she led the way down the hall. She shot the kind of scorching look over her shoulder that was guaranteed to send all the blood in his brain rushing southward.

Maybe he should force the serious talk tonight, but he couldn't do it. Not yet. The closeness they'd rediscovered was too good. He wanted to hold on to it for just a little longer, and they would see each other back home. There were legal—and possible genetic—entanglements left to handle, and he'd be dropping by to visit, even if she didn't realize it yet.

This was not the end. Not even close.

So, he should relax and take advantage of the intimacy she was offering now. It was more than obvious she was going to resist his attempts to become a part of her life again once they returned home. Karen was usually pretty easygoing, but when she decided to be stubborn, it was nearly impossible to change her mind. He was up to the challenge though. The rest of his life depended on it.

They entered her room and he locked the door behind them, then he leaned back against the wood surface. She reached into a small box sitting on top of the dresser and pulled something green from it. When she turned toward him, she was holding an emerald lace teddy against herself. It was barely-there and the mental picture of her wearing it that his imagination sent him made his erection harder than steel in seconds.

"What do you think?" She ran her tongue along her lower lip, her gaze skimming down to his fly, where she had to see the evidence of his lust straining the confines of his zipper.

"I think...I need to see you in it." His voice came out a husky rasp, need roughening his tone. "And I think I owe Valentina a thank you note."

A throaty chuckle was her reply to that. "I'll be right back."

She disappeared into the bathroom, and he let his head drop against the door. He closed his eyes, wishing this trip would never end. It was idyllic here—no future, no past, just this moment. But his moments were slipping away, and the fantasy would end. Returning to reality meant rectifying years of mistakes. Somehow.

Hinges squeaked and he turned to look. His heart stopped, then hammered against his ribs. His imagination had nothing on the real thing. The lace cupped every curve like a lover. He could see the outline of her nipples, and the shadowy triangle of curls between her legs. The neckline plunged into a vee so deep it bared her navel, and there were cut-outs at each hip. Dear God. Fire settled low in his gut, and his body throbbed with painful need. He wanted to bury his face in her lush cleavage and kiss every inch of her creamy flesh.

"You are the most beautiful thing I've ever seen," he breathed.

"The sluttiest thing, you mean." She flushed, though her expression was pleased. She ran a fingertip up a delicate strap that seemed to defy gravity in holding the sheer material in place.

"No." He shook his head. "Incredibly beautiful, unbelievably sexy, absolutely amazing."

Glancing away, she swallowed. "You don't have to say things like that, Tate."

"I say them because I mean them." He was across the room in two strides and set his hands on her hips. "I was a fool to have ever let you go, Karen."

Before she could respond, he covered her mouth with his, shoving his tongue between her lips. She moaned, her fingers fisting in his shirtfront. He skimmed his palms over her back and down to cup the globes of her ass. The textured lace was both soft and stimulating, and wickedness twisted through him as he realized how that might feel on the more intimate portions of her anatomy. He moved one hand around so he could fondle her breast, rubbing the fabric back and forth over her beaded nipple. The other hand dipped between her legs from behind, pressing the lace into her wet sex. She arched in his arms and her teeth sank into his upper lip, scraping over the sensitive flesh. He shuddered, pain and pleasure twisting viciously inside him.

He pulled back, dropped to his knees, jerked the lace aside, and buried his face between her thighs. She squeaked, rising onto tiptoes, but he was relentless, sucking and licking her slick lips. The taste of her cream was a heady aphrodisiac, and her hands tugging at his hair only urged him on.

Little gasps and mewls spilled from her, and she pressed her hips tighter to him. "Tate. Oh my...oh. Tate!"

Her knees buckled and he caught her close, cradling her to his chest. He hooked his fingers into the shoulder straps, pulling them away. "I need you, Karen. I need you."

She wriggled, helping him strip the teddy off her succulent body. Then she reached for the hem of his shirt and tugged it up and over his head. Her fingers spread over his chest and toyed with his nipples. A harsh sound wrenched from deep within him, white-hot lava burning through him. He slipped out his wallet and the condom inside, then wrestled open his fly and pushed his pants down, sitting back to kick his legs free.

After grabbing the rubber from him, she quickly sheathed his erection. He scrambled to his feet, scooped her up and tossed her onto the bed. Her surprised laugh cut short as she bounced against the mattress. Then he was on top of her, sliding into the hot, satin depths of her sex. They both groaned when he was seated fully within her. Nothing, nothing in the world felt as good as being with her, connecting on a physical, emotional level that was so *right*.

He pulled back until he almost slipped from her body, then sank in again and again and again. Time stretched out until there was only her, only this. Right here, right now, she was his whole world, his everything. That was how he wanted it to stay. He tried to show her without words, used every ounce of knowledge and expertise he'd gained over the years to give her pleasure. Slow rotations of his pelvis against her, angling so he hit just the right spot inside her.

"This is awesome," she gasped. A laugh bubbled out of her throat, her hips rising to meet his at each downward thrust. Her cheeks were flushed with passion, her lips curled in an impish grin, her eyes sparkling. A carnal angel going up in flames in his embrace. He adored seeing this side of her, the side no one else ever got to see, the hidden fire that burned under the cool, calm surface.

He framed her face in his palms, stroking his thumbs over the smooth curves of her cheekbones. "You're so damn lovely, sweetheart."

"Tate," she whispered, her expression tender as she reached up to caress his jaw.

Emotion shone in her green gaze, and he'd swear he could feel her love wrap around him. The moment was so perfect, so exactly like it used to be. He couldn't hold back anymore—his control shattered and he was stripped bare. All that was left was the single truth that had shaped his life for over a decade.

"I love you, Karen. I love you so much. I need you forever."

The words hit her like a ton of bricks, ecstasy and agony ripping through her at once. But he kept moving, kept thrusting, and her body simply reacted, her mind shutting down, feeling overruling logic. He hammered deep, grinding down on her, and she exploded into intense climax. Every muscle inside her clenched and released, goose bumps broke over her skin and her channel milked the length of his erection. The hair on his chest rasped over her nipples, the head of his shaft probing her G-spot with each swift plunge, and sensation swamped her, pushing her into one peak after another.

"I love you," he whispered, and then slammed even deeper than he had before, sending them both spinning over into orgasm. He groaned, shuddered over her. A scream wrenched out of her, her back bowing as she came hard, and tears slipped from the corners of her eyes.

Emotion erupted like a volcano within her, and sobs made her chest hitch in rough spasms. She shoved at his shoulders, pushing him off her so she could roll away. She clamped a hand over her mouth and curled into a ball on the side of the mattress.

Oh God. Oh. God. She couldn't believe he'd said that to her. How could he? How dare he make her feel this way? *He had no right!* Every worry and fear from the past week ripped at her soul, all the pain of the last eight years burning her heart like acid until she felt scoured from the inside out. Tate put a hand on her shoulder, and she jerked away from the touch. There was concern in his voice when he spoke, but she didn't hear his words, curled deeper into herself and just cried.

Because Valentina was so right. Karen did still love him, and she hated herself for that weakness, hated that someone who'd hurt her and rejected her so often and for so long was still the one man who owned her soul. What was wrong with her? How much more pathetic could she possibly be?

She didn't know how much time had passed, but when she resurfaced from her misery, she found Tate stroking her hair, crooning wordless comfort. Hiccups rattled her chest, but she forced herself upright, swinging her legs over the side of the bed. She swiped at the dampness on her cheeks. The mattress bounced as Tate moved, and then a tissue appeared in front of her face. She grabbed it and blew her nose.

"Thanks." Her voice came out watery and fainter than she liked. She cleared her throat, wincing at how raw it was.

He settled beside her, close, but not so close he touched her. "I think it's time to talk, whether either of us likes it or not."

The protests that sprang to her lips would only make her sound like a petulant child, so she sniffled and dabbed at her eyes, keeping her mouth shut.

Sighing, he rubbed a hand down his face. "We've both done pretty well at avoiding the serious discussion, but clearly keeping our thoughts to ourselves isn't helping either of us."

Sidestepping the fact that he'd dropped the L-bomb, she went with the topic she'd held back. "I might be pregnant. My period is late. I'll take a test when I get home."

"You could take one here." He gave her an incisive glance, but his tone was non-demanding.

Finding out she was pregnant would send her into an emotional freefall, and she just couldn't handle it right now. She needed a safety net when she took that fall. "I want my friends there when I find out for sure. I know it's stupid, but—"

"No." He set a hand on her shoulder. "This is a huge thing we're facing. Your friends have been with you through everything, giving you support. I wish I could say I had done that for you too, but I didn't. Hell, lately I was the reason you needed their support." Self-loathing colored his voice, and his hand fell away. She hated that she felt bereft without his touch. He sighed. "So, we won't know anything concrete until we're back. That's okay. I understand."

"Thank you," she said stiffly. She resented his kindness, how sad was that?

That penetrating glance speared her again. "I'd like the chance to be there for you in the future, Karen. To make up for how I haven't been there for you before."

The breath clogged in her throat. She squeaked, "I…"

"This time in Rome has been amazing, but I want more than an affair. I want us to get back together." The sincerity in his voice tugged at her heartstrings. "I love you."

There. He'd said it again. She jerked as if he'd slapped her, then shoved to her feet. "No."

"That was a knee-jerk response, Karen." He rose as well, holding up placating hands. "Please, think about it before you reject the idea out of hand. We're good together on so many levels. You have to know that."

She didn't have to know anything. Temper exploded within her, an anger she'd struggled with for years. It tangled with the stabbing pain that hit her when she recalled every instance where she hadn't been important enough to be worth his time.

"So what? You think you can just go back to how it was?" She pounded a fist against his shoulder, and it wasn't nearly enough to vent her agony, so she did it again. And again. And again. Until he caught her arms and pinned them against his chest.

"No, I don't think I can go back. I want us to go forward, together."

"That's quite a flip from the man who ruined our marriage. You threw us away!" Unable to move, she resorted to an acidic hiss. "How could you, Tate? How could you do that to us, to me? What did I ever do to deserve being ignored, forgotten, and slotted dead last on your priority list? Seriously, I think I ranked below mowing the damn lawn."

"No." His throat worked, and moisture filled his eyes. "My priorities were so backwards for so long, but my head is on straight now. Nothing will ever rank above you again. I swear."

"Empty promises," she growled. "Maybe you quit your dad's firm, but you'll start yours and get immersed in your cases and *poof*. Who's Karen? Why does this needy bitch keep yelling at me to give her attention?"

His eyes widened, shock, horror, and grief reflecting in the dark depths. "It was never like that!"

"Wasn't it? That's how it looked from where I was standing." She jerked away from him, shoving her fingers through her short locks. "What does it matter? All this week was about was sex. It was good, but I'm done. I walked away before and I was stupid enough to let myself get sucked back in, but I am done."

"No, please. Please, Karen." He licked his lips, desperation stamped on his features. "Let me prove I can be the man—"

"Why? Why bother? Why open myself up to the endless torture?" She threw her hands out. "I already know I can't be near you and not react, not care. So I just can't be near you. You're like waving a shot glass of whiskey under an alcoholic's nose. It's never going to end well."

"Don't say that."

"It's the truth." Even if she needed to remind herself of that over and over and over again. She'd thought she could have a simple affair with him, but she'd been so wrong, so stupid. There was nothing simple about her feelings for him. They overwhelmed her, and that petrified her. What she'd once welcomed, she now feared.

"No." He reached out a hand and she scrambled back a step.

If he touched her now, she would lose it. She might even give in to the temptation he offered, though she knew it would be the dumbest thing she could do. If she went back to him and he betrayed her again, she would be shattered. There would be no recovery from that. It was a risk she couldn't take, no matter what her heart wanted. Her heart was stupid. It had already proven it couldn't be trusted.

She grabbed a pillow from the bed and used it to cover her nudity. "Please leave."

"Karen."

The pleading in his voice almost broke her, but she firmed her chin and dug deep for some resolve. "Just go. I have to protect myself—I deserve better than you'll ever be able to give me."

He swiped at his eyes before tears could escape, but his voice shook. "Maybe that was true in the past, but I've changed."

She pressed her lips together to quell a sob, shook her head, and pointed toward the door. "Go, damn it!"

"I love you. I'm sorry." And then he was gone.

Crumpling to the mattress, she could still smell him on the sheets. Pain spread like an aching bruise inside her. This was so much worse than the first time they'd split up. Then, he'd just let her leave, never saying a word to stop her.

Now, he'd spent a week using their shared history of a city they both loved to remind her of all the qualities she'd fallen for in the first place—his humor, his kindness, his easy companionship, his ability to turn her on with a single glance. She'd missed those things, and it had felt so good to have them back, to be near him again. His campaign had been far more effective than she wanted to admit, but she had to be strong. Somehow.

Because, God help her, she still had to deal with the fact that his child might even now be growing in her womb.

CHAPTER ELEVEN

T ate climbed into his car and stared out the windshield for a moment. It had been six days since he'd returned from Rome—six long, agonizing days, six empty, sleepless nights. He'd reached for Karen so many times, but she wasn't there. Letting a heavy breath filter out of his lungs, he slipped his key in the ignition and fired up the engine. He'd given her some time and space to think, hoped she'd get in touch—if for no other reason than to let him know if she was having their baby—but she hadn't.

So, now he needed to gird his loins and try again.

He blinked when the passenger door opened and his sister plopped herself into the seat. "Oh, good. You can drive me to the Stanford gallery."

"There's public transportation that would take you right to campus," he pointed out.

"Yeah, but I'm late, and I'd rather not run to catch a bus." She snapped on her seatbelt. "There's only one thing worth sweating for, and running isn't it."

"Say no more. Really." Following suit, he clipped his seatbelt into place. "That's all the detail I need on that topic."

"You're welcome," she replied cheerfully. "So, where are you going?"

He backed out of the driveway and headed toward the gallery. "I'm having a real estate agent show me some potential office spaces."

She smirked. "And would these offices be located in Half Moon Bay, brother dear?"

"They would be, yes." He'd also discussed putting the Palo Alto house on the market. Even if Karen didn't take him back, he couldn't live there without her. The memories would haunt him forever. He needed a fresh start on every possible level—personal and professional.

"Ballsy, I like it." Admiration shone in Laurel's voice, but after a short pause she added, "You do realize she turned you down though, right?"

His sister knew all about what had gone down in Italy. She'd shown up at the airport—driving his car—and had pried a confession out of him before they were halfway back from SFO. For the first time in his life, he agreed with his parents. It was too bad she'd become an artist because she'd make a terrifyingly good lawyer.

"Whether she turned me down or not is irrelevant. If she's pregnant, she's going to need help. I want to be there for her and for our child."

She flipped down the mirror and finger-combed her purple-tipped hair. "You're that sure she's pregnant?"

"I'm that hopeful she's pregnant," he corrected. The lack of news had been driving him slowly mad. He didn't know what that might mean. That Karen wasn't pregnant or that she was pregnant and wasn't ready to tell him yet? It could go either way.

He turned onto University Avenue and sat through the many lights and obnoxious gridlocked traffic that were indicative of this part of town.

Laurel's fingers tapped a quick tattoo on her thigh. Always in motion, that was his sister. "You're not going to give up on winning her back, are you?"

"Nope." It was going to batter the hell out of his soul to go through another confrontation like they'd had in Rome, but Karen was worth any hoop he had to jump through.

"She's allowed to say no, you know." His sister twisted in her seat to face him. "Even if she's knocked up."

"I know." He drove through the Stanford campus toward the building with the gallery. "But I think she's just running scared now. She doesn't know how to trust me or how to trust herself with me." He held up his hand when she opened her mouth to comment. "Yeah, I deserve that distrust. But I'll never convince her there's nothing to be scared of if I give up at the first sign of resistance."

Exactly when he'd give up, he didn't know. But he'd seen the conflict in Karen's gaze when she told him to leave. It gave him hope that he might still save this marriage. She'd admitted she couldn't be near him and not care for him, so he needed to be near her and foster those feelings. He doubted she'd make it easy on him, but he didn't deserve easy. Then again, as Laurel had said, he did deserve to be happy.

His sister leaned over and popped a kiss on his jaw. "I'm rooting for you, bro. But if you fuck up again and hurt her, I'll hold you down and let her kick your ass."

"Thanks," he drawled as he pulled up to the curb in front of the gallery. "Your faith and support gives me this warm, fuzzy feeling inside. Kind of like mold."

Snorting, she patted his cheek. "Love you."

"Love you too." He hit the button to pop the door locks and shot her a pointed glance. "Now get out of my car."

"Bye!" She laughed and hopped out, giving him a jaunty wave as she disappeared into the building.

Within minutes, he was back on his way to Half Moon Bay. On his way to the future, whatever it might hold.

I t turned out Karen didn't need to take a pregnancy test. She started her period on the flight home from Italy. Six days later, it was over, but she still hadn't managed to call Tate.

She'd gone home from work to eat lunch, but her best friends surprised her by showing up with take-out from her favorite Thai place. They'd hovered protectively since she'd gotten back. Normally that would annoy her, but she couldn't say she minded now. She needed to feel not so alone in the world. With her parents still on their road trip and her brother away at college, that left her friends to fill in the gap. Which they'd done.

Unlocking the door, she let them inside. They all had keys, but they stood back and let her do the honors. Then they spilled into the apartment and gathered around her coffee table.

Rifling through the bags showed they'd ordered Pad Thai for her. "Ah, you guys do love me."

"We really do." Meg gave her a wink and handed out plastic forks to everyone.

They dug into the food, and it was delicious. Much better than the peanut butter and jelly sandwich Karen had planned to slap together for lunch.

Julie swallowed a bite of noodles. "How's the new job going?"

"It's only my second day, but so far, so good." Karen rocked her hand back and forth through the air. "Still working off the jetlag though. My sleeping hours resemble a ninety-year-old grandmother's."

Her friends exchanged glances, and of course it was Anne who voiced whatever was on their minds. "Speaking of getting back to normal...have you gotten around to telling Tate he's not going to be your baby-daddy?"

"No." The food seemed to congeal in Karen's belly, and she set aside the carton. "I know I need to tell him. Just get it over with."

Anne grabbed Karen's cell from her purse and handed it over. "Do it now, while we're here. It'll be easier that way."

She stared down at her phone for a long moment, emotion tightening her throat. "I just... This will be the end of it, then. Done. Over."

"If you don't want it to be the end, it doesn't have to be." Julie squeezed her free hand. "I'm pretty sure if you said the word, Tate would be on your doorstep so fast he'd leave skid marks all the way from Palo Alto."

And that was a tempting thought, wasn't it? Then again, she hadn't thought of much else since she'd kicked him out of her hotel room. He wanted another shot at marriage with her. He still loved her. God, that was sweet and painful all at once. But her reaction had been knee-jerk, hadn't it? He'd been dead right about that. Still, dwelling on it for days hadn't brought her any closer to figuring out what she wanted.

She shook her head, tapped his name in her contacts list and was sent immediately to his voicemail. So, he was either out of range for reception or had his phone turned off. It was a relief not to have to speak to him directly, but leaving a message about this kind of topic felt weird too.

Swallowing hard, she forced the words out. "Hi, Tate. It's Karen. I just wanted to let you know that I'm...I'm not p-pregnant." The last word cracked, and she rushed to get the rest out while she still could. "So, you don't have to worry about adding custody stuff to our divorce agreement. Just...wanted you to know. Bye."

And wasn't that the most pathetic voicemail to have to leave? Tears started leaking down her cheeks the second she hung up, and her friends piled in for a group hug.

"I am such an idiot." Her voice emerged half moan, half whimper. "I really thought I was...that we'd..."

The grief of not being pregnant overwhelmed her again. Not until she'd realized she wasn't had she truly understood how very much she'd wanted his child. Mistake or not, she would have loved that baby *so much*.

"No, no." Meg rocked her a bit. "Wanting to have his kid doesn't make you an idiot. At least this way you would have known the dad. There's nothing wrong with that."

Karen clenched her teeth to try to hold in a sob. "But I shouldn't want anything to do with him anymore. We're divorcing."

"Loving him doesn't make you stupid, honey." Julie rubbed a hand up and down her back, forced cheer in her voice. "And, hey, if Lukas can give love a second try, anyone can. His first wife was mentally ill. At least we know Tate is sane."

A snuffling laugh erupted from Karen. "Yeah, he's sane."

"And hot," Anne added. She leaned back when everyone gave her a look. "What? You've all thought it too! Also, a solid sense of humor is good. But, you know, a muffiny ass doesn't hurt."

"Anne!" Meg reached over and swatted the redhead's arm.

"I stand by my previous statements," Anne said austerely, smoothing a hand down her sleeve.

"Look, sweetie." Meg leaned forward, her gaze serious. "If you honestly don't want him back, that's one thing. But if you're not taking him back because you're scared you'll get hurt again... Honey, I've been there, and I almost lost Finn because I was too afraid to try again. Don't let your fear run your life. Any guy you're with will hurt you, and you'll hurt him. That's how relationships work, but the good stuff makes it worth it when you're with the right person."

"So the question is...is Tate the right person for me now? Maybe. Maybe not. I haven't figured that out yet." But that was the first time Karen had admitted aloud that, yes, he might still be the right guy for her. She sat back and sighed. "I need to get back to the library."

"Are you sure you don't want to call in sick or something?" Julie asked. "You can keep me company at the yarn shop."

Shaking her head, Karen closed the lid on her leftovers. "I'd rather be distracted from...everything."

"If you need company after work, come to dinner at my place." Meg gave Karen's knee an encouraging pat. "Finn would be happy to see you too."

Anne grinned cheekily. "Or you could come over to my place and let the drama llama drive you up the wall. Then you'll feel so much better about all your life choices."

"Wow, that's quite an offer." Karen's laugh was a bit ragged.

"You know me—I'm here for ya, babe." Anne shoved her empty food container into a plastic bag.

"Thanks. I think." Karen managed a smile.

"You don't have to be alone, if you don't want to." Julie took Karen's leftovers to the fridge, then helped tidy up the rest of lunch. "Lukas is out of town at an academic conference, so if you want quiet time, come to my house. We can watch bad movies and eat our weight in ice cream."

Ice cream just reminded Karen of gelato, which reminded her of

Tate. Bad movies reminded her of him too. Everything reminded her of Tate now. She sighed, her smile fading. Without the possibility of a child, she had to be totally honest with herself about what she wanted. There was no blaming anything on the baby—if Tate was allowed back into her life, it was because she decided to make it that way, not because a child forced them into contact.

Hours later, she was still in her new office, immersed in work. She let go of all her problems and focused on the library budget for the year and how funds were going to be allocated—print books, electronic books, programming events, staffing. Everything was on her shoulders here, and she wanted to do her job well.

A swift knock made her door vibrate in its frame. She kept her eyes on her screen to finish the function she was inserting into her spreadsheet. "Just a second!"

Instead of heeding her, Tate walked in and shut the door, then wrapped her up in his arms and held her tight. "I'm so sorry, sweetheart."

The emotional rollercoaster of the last few weeks hit her with the subtle force of a sledgehammer. Being in his embrace again was so reassuring, so secure, so right. A sob broke from her throat, and she tried to push away from him, but he wouldn't let her go. She'd spent far too much time crying lately, and she was at work. "Don't...I can't..."

"I'm disappointed too."

"You are?" The raw pain in his voice stunned her, took the fight out of her. He'd never said anything about wanting kids, not the way she had.

"Yes. I was really hoping we'd made a baby." He rocked her gently, and she let him, took the comfort he offered because she needed it so badly.

After a few minutes, she pulled back, swiping at her damp cheeks.

"Why are you in Half Moon Bay? You didn't come here just to give me a hug."

Though if she were honest, she wouldn't mind the sentiment of that, impractical as it was.

He arched his eyebrows and settled into the chair across from her desk. "Just visiting the public library in my new hometown."

"Your new... What?" She gaped at him like a moron.

His gaze followed her as she walked around and flopped into her chair. His broad shoulder dipped in a shrug. "My new hometown. I just leased an office space. I'm looking at a couple of apartments to rent while I wait for the Palo Alto house to sell. Do you like your complex?"

"You're relocating your life? Here?" She felt like she'd walked into the middle of a conversation and had no idea what was going on. She'd turned him down on reconciliation—no matter how she might be reconsidering—and he'd clearly gotten her voicemail, so what he was telling her made no sense. "I don't understand. Why do that? I'm not pregnant."

"So we'll try again."

She sputtered.

"Ah, you thought when you kicked me out of your room in Rome that I'd stay gone, huh?" He hitched his ankle onto his opposite knee. "Sorry. Nope."

Maybe it was time to reassess that whole sanity thing. "Uh...have you lost your mind?"

"Actually, I have a clarity I haven't felt in years." He steepled his fingers together and a small smile touched his lips. "It's an amazing feeling, really."

The familiar powerlessness flooded her. She'd felt this way during her marriage—like she had no say, no control. Nothing was ever on her terms. Her eyes narrowed to dangerous slits. "Didn't I make it clear I can't be around you? I have the right to kick you out of my life if I want to."

His expression sobered and he nodded. "Laurel said the same thing, and it's true. But I have the right to fight for what I believe in. And I believe in us. I believe we are the best possible life partners for each other."

"It takes two to make a relationship." She folded her arms. "Maybe that's something you never figured out."

"Do you still love me?"

The question rocked her down to her foundation. No, he was *not* taking control of this conversation by laying her emotions bare. "That's none of your business. I'm not your wife anymore."

"Actually, you are." His tone was deceptively mild when he delivered a killing blow. "I haven't signed the divorce papers."

She stared at him so long he started to fidget, and she had to admit she liked discomfiting him. "You're going to drag me through an ugly divorce? After practically shoving me out of your life, you're going to make me suffer for leaving. That's low, Tate."

"No, that's not what I meant. It's just...I never..." He rubbed a hand over the back of his neck. He closed his eyes for a moment, sighed, then met her gaze directly. "We're good together, Karen. We love each other. We can make this work."

The utter certainty in his voice almost swayed her, but it wasn't enough that he was convinced. She had to be certain too. So, she laid it on the line for him. "I'm not sure I'd survive getting my heart trampled again in the name of your ambition."

"I swear that won't happen." The words were a low, soothing rumble. His fingertips tapped his chest. "I *swear* your heart is safe with me this time."

Maybe it was, maybe it wasn't. She didn't want fears to make her decisions for her, but blind faith wasn't something she could manage. Not after all he'd put her through. "I don't know how to believe you."

It helped that his voice was completely non-defensive, his body language open, his expression a mixture of remorse and entreaty. "I will do whatever it takes to earn back your trust and keep it, Karen. I fucked up. Over and over again. I have no real excuses, no justifications. I. Fucked. Up." His chest rose and fell in a huge sigh. "But I've seen what life is like without you, and it sucks. It's just…empty. It's going through the motions and not really caring about anything. I hated every second of it."

Yes, a tiny part of her liked that he'd been miserable without her. It helped make up—just a little—for the misery she'd felt. "You didn't want me when you had me."

"Yes, I did." He leaned in, set his palm on the desktop. "I didn't show it very well, but I did want you. I have always, *always* wanted you."

She let her head fall back against her chair. Time to really figure it out. What did she want? Yes, she'd left him, but her heart hadn't quite let him go yet. Rome had shown her that the young man she'd fallen for was still there, but the mature version of Tate—once he was out of the office—ah, he was even more irresistible than his college-aged self. Now that Tate, the grown-up, not-obsessed-with-work Tate, was the man she wanted to be married to.

But could he stay that man back here in the real world? People were different on vacation. So, the question was, did she want to take the chance that he'd revert to the Mini-Robert she'd been shackled to for eight years? She was scared of what might happen, how badly it could fall apart, but she managed to set the fear aside for a moment. Logic told her no guy would ever fit her as well as he did. Plus, she loved him. Down to her bones love.

Holding on to that was worth the risk. Terrifying, yes, but worth it.

Because a lawyer never stopped arguing, he filled the silence with more persuasion. "Gio said that a love like ours is worth fighting for, and he was right. So that's what I'm doing. I let you walk away once, and I'm not doing that again. The regret might just kill me. So here I am, and here I'm going to be. Because we are good together. Because we love each other."

"I never said I still loved you," she pointed out. What? She couldn't make it that easy for him.

He gave her a lopsided smile. "You don't have to say it. Not until you're ready. You said you couldn't be around me without caring. I'll take that."

Oh yeah. This man knew her far too well. Also scary, but also good. "Tate—"

After pushing to his feet, he came around her desk and knelt beside her. She swiveled to face him, and he took her hands. "I know I hurt you, and I know you're worried I'll do it again, but I won't. I don't expect you to believe me yet. But I'm still going to be here a week from now, a month, a year. Telling you I'm sorry I was such an idiot, telling you how much I love you, begging you for just one more chance. I don't care if it takes me another eight years to convince you. I'm not going anywhere."

Her tone was dry when she said, "That's stalking and harassment and...probably forty-five other crimes."

"Well, if you feel like taking this to court, I know a good lawyer." His grin was self-effacing and he squeezed her fingers.

She snorted, she couldn't help it. "Smart ass."

"I love you, Karen." His thumbs stroked over the back of her hands, sending little tingles over her skin. "I will love you to my dying day."

Him saying that, on his knees. Now, there was a nice little fantasy come true. "I'm not sure I can—"

His hands tightened on hers. "Trust isn't something that's built overnight, sweetheart, especially once it's been broken. Give me the time, the chance, to convince you."

"What would that entail?" She licked her lips and his gaze shifted to her mouth, awareness shimmered between them, but she refused to let herself be distracted. She tugged on his hands and he met her eyes again.

"Not fighting to keep me out of your life would be a good start. I'll fight just as hard to stay in it, and we'll just hurt each other more. I don't want that, but I can't—*I can't*—stay away." He swallowed hard. "Don't ask it of me. Anything else but that."

She pulled in a slow breath and let it out. There was no denying that she was still scared, still worried. What would it take to make her feel more secure? "Okay, I won't try to keep you out of my life, but I have conditions."

His big body froze as her words hit him, and she saw hope and joy fill his gaze. His fingers clenched on hers painfully. "Name them. Anything."

"First, I want couples counseling. I think we're going to need a referee for a while." She'd asked for this a year before she'd filed for divorce, and he'd flatly refused.

"Done," he stated. "We can find a counselor here in HMB."

Well, that had been the easy condition. The next one he was going to like a lot less. "Second, I want you to sign the divorce papers and give them to me."

Fear spasmed across his face. "Karen."

She didn't back down, kept her expression dead serious. "You said I could ask you for anything. That's what I'm asking. I will give you one more chance and if you mess it up, if you hurt me or make me feel in any way like I'm less important than your work or your father or anyone else, I get to file those papers. That's my deal. Take it or leave it."

A shudder ran through him, a muscle ticking in his jaw. "You'll tell me before you file them?"

"Yes, but you will not fight me on the divorce if you blow this chance." She lifted her eyebrows. "Do we have a deal?"

"Yes. We have a deal." He brought her hand to his lips, turned it over, and kissed her palm. "You won't regret this, Karen. I love you."

She tugged her hands away, then cupped his face. "I love you too, and that's the only reason you're getting this last shot. You're lucky we had Rome."

His eyes looked a bit damp, and a beautiful, tender smile curved his mouth. It was the smile that had always been just for her, that told her how precious she was to him. She'd always loved that smile.

He leaned into her touch. "I will always be grateful for Rome. Because it gave you to me the first time, and then gave you back to me when I was foolish enough to let you go. It's my favorite city in the world. Though I have a feeling this one is going to be a close second."

Pushing her chair back, she rose and he scrambled to his feet. His hands twitched as if he wanted to grab her. Afraid she'd make a run for it? She guessed they both had some worries to work through. They'd have to do that together. That felt right, and some of the tension seeped out of her. They could do this, if they wanted to, if they were willing to put in the effort. But they both had to be all in. That was the most terrifying part, but the payoff if things went well? Priceless.

She tipped her head back to meet his gaze. "So, you leased an office, huh?"

"Yes, I did." He stroked her hair away from her face, and she realized how much she'd missed his hands on her.

Her lips twisted, and she hesitated before she put voice to her next thought. "Are you thinking about buying a house here or just renting for now?"

"Buying." His penetrating gaze speared her. "Why? Is there a house you want?"

"There's this big old Victorian with a huge yard, right on the beach. It used to be an inn, but went under a couple of years ago and no one's bought it." She shrugged. "I always loved walking by it as a kid, but it probably needs serious renovations."

"That's what contractors are for," he said reasonably. "It can't hurt to look."

She fished her purse out of a desk drawer. "Okay, we can look."

"Right now?" Hopefulness lilted his words. "I can call the realtor that showed me my new office. I'm sure she'd be happy to show us any house. When are you off work?"

"Um." She glanced at the clock in the corner of her computer screen. "An hour ago. I'm still getting my bearings."

Quickly saving her spreadsheet, she shut down for the night. It was past time to go.

Empathy darkened his brown eyes. "And you have nothing to go home to, so why bother? I know that feeling all too well."

She poked a finger at his shoulder. "I'm not agreeing to move in with you yet. I'm just saying there's a house I like."

"Understood."

His reply was so swift, she almost grinned. "If I asked for a pony right now, you'd go for it, wouldn't you?"

One eyebrow arched. "What color pony?"

She did grin then. He smiled back, and her heart skipped a beat. Hope tangled with uncertainty. This was going to be hard. She wouldn't lie to herself about that. Rebuilding trust was going to be a rough road to travel for both of them.

She slung her purse strap over her shoulder, heading for the door. She turned back just before she reached it. "Tate?"

"Yeah?" He must have sensed some of her feelings, because he immediately pulled her into his arms. She sighed, relaxing against him.

Honesty was going to need to be a big part of their relationship recovery, so she met his gaze and admitted, "I'm scared."

He let his forehead drop to meet hers, never breaking eye contact. "Me too. Scared I'll screw this up, scared I'm going to get my heart dropkicked if you change your mind."

"I love you," she whispered.

He kissed her then, and their lips clung. It was slow and soft and just right. Their tongues twined and they explored each other, so much love and longing in the kiss that it made her heart squeeze. Warmth swirled inside her, rising to a wicked heat. She ran her hands over him, outlining every muscle and curve with her fingertips. It was as if years had passed since she'd touched him, rather than a few days. He seemed just as unable to stop himself from stroking her body. His fingers sifted through her short hair, cradling the back of her head while he scraped his teeth over her lower lip. She moaned low in her throat when he gently broke the contact.

"I love you, Karen." His voice shook with emotion. "You are the most important thing in my life, and I will never give you a reason to believe otherwise. I promise."

She balled her fingers in the front of his polo shirt. "I'm holding you to that."

The smile she loved lit his face. "Do that."

EPILOGUE

Eight months later...

Tate had kept all his promises. Every single one of them. He'd kept his client list restricted so he could come home to Karen every day at a reasonable hour. He'd taken on two partners so that he could share the workload, and so that he didn't feel the need to control every detail the way his father did. He'd flatly refused to let Robert draw him back into any of the cases at the Patton family firm.

And he had reminded her every single day that he loved her, that he'd learned his lesson very well, that she was the most precious part of his life.

He'd also managed to knock her up, but he didn't know that yet. That was her little surprise to him. A housewarming gift, since they were finally moving into the renovated inn. It had been in rough shape, but working with the contractors to restore it had given her something to talk to Tate about at times when she'd struggled against lashing out from old angers, when the fear of how badly he could hurt her again had almost let her shove him out of her life for good.

They'd seen a counselor for the first couple of months, and he'd been on time for every single appointment. No excuses, no letting anything else get in the way. There were a lot of days at first that had been touch and go, but he'd held on, just as he'd said he would. He'd taken everything she'd dished out until the pockets of bitterness that she'd had to excise had disappeared one by one.

Rain pattered against the window of one of the smaller bedrooms on the second floor. She already had plans to make the room a nursery. Leaning against the windowsill, she watched Tate jog from the woodshed to the house, his arms piled with logs for the fire. Happiness expanded inside her until she just couldn't contain it, and a smile burst across her lips.

The holidays were right around the corner, and she couldn't believe the changes a single year wrought. Last Christmas, they'd broken up. This Christmas, she couldn't imagine her life without him. And life was pretty damn good.

Her friends and family would be over later for an unpacking party, which would be a lot more joyous than the last one she'd had at her apartment. Francesca intended to put in an appearance—she'd been surprisingly supportive of Tate's career shift. Robert was busy with work tonight, of course. Tate's sister would show up too, and Laurel combined with Anne promised to be an outrageous and hilarious time.

But right now, Karen was content to spend her first few hours in her new home with just her husband for company. She heard the front door slam and then his footsteps thudded against the stairs. She left the future nursery and joined him in the master suite, where he was stacking logs in the grate.

"I'm glad you brought some wood in. I thought we could break in the fireplace now." After walking over to a box shoved against the wall, she rifled through it until she found what she was looking for.

"Sure." He reached for the matchbook sitting on the mantel. "I think I know which box downstairs has marshmallows in it, if you want to roast some."

"Marshmallows are good." She held out a folded sheaf of papers. "You can use this as kindling."

She watched comprehension break over his face as he realized she was offering him the signed divorce papers. His eyes widened and his mouth fell open. The silence was so complete she could hear every breath he took.

So many emotions flickered across his expression, she couldn't pinpoint them all. He swallowed. "You don't have to. If it makes you feel safer—"

"It doesn't. It did. But I don't need it anymore." And she didn't. He'd worked his ass off to convince her that he was a changed man, and she'd seen the truth herself. She felt it every time he touched her, smiled at her, came home to her on time. He'd more than proven himself, and...she trusted him. It was that simple. "All I need is you. I love you, Tate."

T ate's heart just stopped. Disbelief and hope flooded him. A tremor ran through his fingers as he reached for the papers she proffered. "Are you really sure?"

Her green gaze shone with love and she nodded. "I adore you. More importantly, I have faith in you, in our marriage. If we run into more problems, I trust that we can make it through them. We're in this together. No more divorce petition needed."

He tossed the sheaf on top of the firewood, then offered her the matchbook. "Why don't you do the honors?"

She didn't hesitate, striking a match and setting the papers on fire. She dusted her hands off, nodding in satisfaction. "There."

Gratitude flooded him. Thank God he'd gone on that impromptu trip to Rome. Thank God Karen had been there too and he'd been smart enough to ask her for another shot at marriage. Thank God he'd escaped the family law firm. He'd never been the type to count on coincidence, but so many pieces had fallen into exactly the right place at exactly the right time, he couldn't call it anything other than fate or destiny or plain, dumb luck. He was just so damn glad for all of it.

After pulling her into his embrace, he buried his face into the crook of her neck, breathing in her sweet scent. "Thank you."

"My pleasure." She rubbed a hand up and down his back in slow sweeps.

"I meant...thank you for giving me a second chance." He leaned back to look at her. "Thank you."

"You made the most of the opportunity, Patton." Her grin was cheeky and she reached up to tweak his chin. "Good job."

A short laugh spilled out of him. "Awesome."

"I can make your day even better." Secrets danced in her gaze, and dimples tucked into the corners of her mouth.

He shook his head. "There's no way today could be any better."

"Yeah, it could." She grabbed his hand and moved it down to lie against the curve of her belly.

It took him a moment to get the message, but when it did, his knees actually went weak. She was pregnant. They were having a baby. He was going to be a father. "Holy shit."

"Yep, that was my thought too." She chuckled, delight shining in her eyes. "Two pink lines on the pregnancy test this morning. Holy shit."

Pure joy and utter contentment wound through him. The last few months had been the finest of his life. When Karen had left a year ago, he couldn't even conceive of being happy again. But this...this was as close to perfect as he'd ever been. The future looked amazing—his wife back in his life, a baby on the way. The new house and thriving law practice were just icing on the cake.

"You're right, sweetheart. It's even better now. The best day of my life."

THE END

Want a sneak peek at how Tate originally proposed to Karen? Join C. Jordan's mailing list for a FREE copy of the bonus prequel short story, *Just This Once*.

https://www.cjordanbooks.com/bonus-content

ABOUT C. JORDAN

C. Jordan is a California native with an insatiable love for travel. When she's not writing sexy contemporary romance, she can usually be found working as a librarian or wandering the world with her husband.

ALSO BY C. JORDAN

EXCErPT FrOM WILD
FOr YOU

Half Moon Bay, California

The final confirmation email had arrived.

It was official: she was booked on an adventure cruise through Alaska's Inner Passages. Three solid weeks of sailing, camping, hiking, kayaking, and ice climbing in some of the most gorgeous wilderness the US had to offer.

This was going to *rock*.

Even an hour later, a huge grin still curled Anne Kirby's lips. She did a little dance step as she crossed Main Street and bounced into the Moonside Café, where she was meeting her three best friends for their weekly dinner.

Karen pressed a palm to her burgeoning belly, using her free hand to wave Anne over. Anne slipped into the seat next to the blonde, where they faced Julie and Meg.

"What's up?" Anne asked. There was an air of tension over the table that made her a bit wary.

"Wedding planning," replied all three of her friends at once.

Yikes. There was a topic guaranteed to give Anne hives. Not something she was ever doing. No way, no how. Hell, no. Even if she ever took the fall for some lucky guy, she was eloping. Somewhere far, far away. Period. She shuddered to think of the mileage for drama her mother would get out of a wedding. Yep, she'd leave that pain and suffering to her little sisters, if they decided to do the full event.

A waitress came by to fill Anne's coffee cup, and she nodded her thanks.

"Back to our conversation." Making an agonized face, Karen glanced at Meg. "The ceremony is still a month away, girlfriend. *Look* at me. I'm huge and I still have seven weeks to go! I can't believe you want a woman who'll be eight-and-a-half-months pregnant as your maid of honor. Not that I'll upstage the bride in prettiness, but I might eclipse you if I turn sideways."

Anne snorted but tried to cover it by taking a sip from her mug. Not that she fooled anyone—her friends knew her too well for that.

"I don't care," Meg replied, her tone emphatic. "I want my friends there with me, even if we have to roll you down the aisle. We're keeping it short, so you won't have to be on your feet long. Besides, I think Finn might die if we did a big, formal, dragged-out ceremony."

"Please," Anne shot back. "That man would crawl over broken glass for you. If you wanted a long, fancy-ass ceremony, he'd let you have it."

A satisfied grin tugged at Meg's lips, and a happy sighed soughed out. "Yeah, he would. I think I'll keep him."

"Blech." The annoyed noise was out of Anne's mouth before she could stop it, and her three friends stared at her. She waved them away. "You guys are just so disgustingly in love. *All three of you*. It's nauseating."

Julie's look was sly. "Jealous, little orphan Annie?"

Oh, now there was a surefire way to piss her off. The fact that she had bright red hair had led to more teasing in her childhood than she cared to recall. Orphan Annie, Anne of Green Gables, Carrot Top, Big Red. The list went on, some more perverted and insulting than others. Her hair couldn't even be a nice shade of auburn like two of her three younger sisters. Nope, Anne's was red. In-your-face *red*.

She scrubbed a hand over her short locks and glared at Julie. "Don't be a jerk."

Julie opened her mouth to retort when Meg poked her in the arm. "Quit antagonizing."

"But that's what I *do.*" Julie's eyes widened. "Someone has to egg you guys on or we'd never have any fun."

"Too bad. You'll adjust," Karen replied unsympathetically, patting her rounded belly.

Movement rippled beneath the surface, which always fascinated and horrified Anne at the same time. She set her palm next to her friend's and felt the baby kick. "The belly alien lives."

The creepy, ominous tone she used made Meg and Julie chortle. Karen just rolled her eyes. "Yes, and the belly alien wants feeding. So unless you want me to sic him on you, you'd better flag down the waitress so we can order."

Anne arched an eyebrow, glancing across the table at her friends. "You know, I think she means it. Pregnancy has turned her cannibalistic. The belly alien's terrifying bloodlust is taking over her body."

Meg flagged down the waitress. "I think it's vampires who have bloodlust, not cannibals."

"Yeah." Karen's smile was not at all reassuring. "Cannibals like their food cooked. They roast 'em live over an open fire first."

Julie raised a finger in the air, her tone turning as pious as any priest's. "Note that I am not the one antagonizing here."

"You're such a good girl," Anne cooed. "We'll be sure to tell Lukas to reward you tonight."

"No need." Julie's grin was positively sinful. "I'll tell him myself."

The waitress appeared with a breadbasket and took their orders. Karen fell on the rolls like she'd never eaten before in her life. She moaned, closing her eyes.

"Okay, while she has a private moment with the bread..." Anne let that thought trail off and reached into her messenger bag. Pulling out the printed email, she slapped it on the table. "Check that out."

Meg and Julie leaned forward. After a moment of silence, Julie squealed. "No way! You did it?"

"What?" Karen craned her neck to see. "Oh my God, you finally booked a trip to Alaska? You've been saying you wanted to go there forever!"

She threw her arm around Anne's shoulders for a quick hug, and Anne couldn't stop a stupid grin from spreading across her face. While she'd been on a million weekend trips to Yosemite, Big Sur, Mount Shasta, and the Sierra Nevadas, she'd always had to stay close enough to home so she could ensure her younger sisters got to school Monday morning. But her youngest sibling had just finished up her freshman year in college and had a summer job in San Francisco, which meant Anne was free to leave town. She'd be back in time for Meg and Finn's wedding at the end of July and the start of the school year in mid-August. She was a gym teacher at the local middle school, so these summer months without any responsibilities were a first. Normally, she spent the whole time refereeing the squabbles between the diametrically opposed personalities of her sisters. But not this year.

"Three whole weeks," she said with relish. "I was going to take the ten-day trip, but they had a last-minute Memorial Day sale and I jumped on it. Three. Freaking. *Weeks.*"

Her friends squealed and enthused and asked questions and Anne could feel a little of the dissatisfaction that had plagued her lately begin to fall away. Yes. This was exactly what she needed. Time to get the hell out of Dodge.

Meg hesitated for a long moment. "I hate to ask but...what did your mom say?"

Ah, yes. Her mom. There was a topic guaranteed to burst her bubble. Dinah Kirby was the biggest drama queen who'd ever lived, and Anne had no idea how she was going to break this to her in a way that wouldn't cause a meltdown. Her mom was codependent on a level that suffocated Anne. It hadn't been so bad with her sisters there to help deflect, but now?

Anne sighed. "I didn't want to tell her until I had something to tell. Until I pushed the buy button, I wasn't sure I was going to do it. So that's what I get to do after dinner."

Julie's expression was compassionate. "My couch is available if she goes atomic on you."

"Thanks. I'll be fine." Or at least, Anne hoped she would. Dinah and she rarely fought—mostly because Anne kept her mouth shut—so this might be a novel experience. Not a *fun* experience, but a novel one. "Really, it'll be fine."

Meg cocked her head. "As long as you don't let her drive you into staying in Alaska forever. I expect you to be back for my wedding." She poked a finger in Karen's direction. "If pregnant lady and the belly alien can't escape, you can't either."

Kicking back in an exaggerated pose of relaxation, Anne folded her hands behind her head. She grinned. "Honey, I'm not just going to be back in time for the wedding, I'll be back in time to make sure you have a bachelorette party you'll never forget."

"If it's anything like the one she threw for me..." Karen's voice trailed off, her eyes rounding with horror.

Anne just let her smile widen in a way she knew would worry them. As it should. Really, there was nothing quite so fun as yanking her best friends' chains.